ALSO BY ALEJANDRO ZAMBRA

Bonsai

The Private Lives of Trees

WAYS OF
GOING HOME

WAYS OF GOING HOME

ALEJANDRO ZAMBRA

TRANSLATED FROM THE SPANISH BY
MEGAN McDOWELL

FARRAR, STRAUS AND GIROUX   NEW YORK

Farrar, Straus and Giroux
18 West 18th Street, New York 10011

A portion of this book originally appeared, in slightly different form, in
Granta 113: Best of Young Spanish-Language Novelists.

Library of Congress Cataloging-in-Publication Data
Zambra, Alejandro, 1975–
    [Formas de volver a casa. English]
    Ways of going home / Alejandro Zambra ; translated from the Spanish by
Megan McDowell. — 1st American ed.
        p.   cm.
    ISBN 978-0-374-28664-4 (alk. paper)
    1. Families—Chile—Fiction.   2. Chilean literature—Translations
into English.   I. McDowell, Megan.   II. Title.

PQ8098.36.A43 F6713 2013
863'.7—dc23

                                                              2012021270

Designed by Abby Kagan

Illustration on title and part title pages by Charlotte Strick

www.fsgbooks.com
www.twitter.com/fsgbooks • www.facebook.com/fsgbooks

1   3   5   7   9   10   8   6   4   2

The author and translator wish to thank Neil Davidson for
his assistance with the translation.

FOR ANDREA

Now I know how to walk; I can no longer learn to walk.

—W. Benjamin

Instead of howling, I write books.
—R. Gary

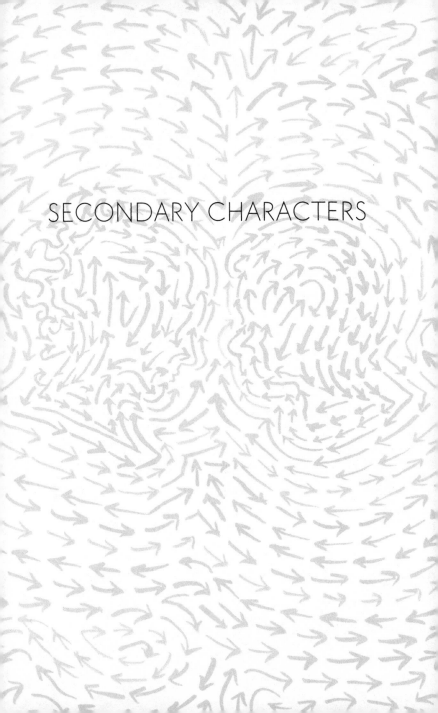

SECONDARY CHARACTERS

ONCE, I GOT LOST. I WAS SIX OR SEVEN. I GOT distracted, and all of a sudden I couldn't see my parents anymore. I was scared, but I immediately found the way home and got there before they did. They kept looking for me, desperate, but I thought that they were lost. That I knew how to get home and they didn't.

"You went a different way," my mother said later, angry, her eyes still swollen.

You were the ones who went a different way, I thought, but I didn't say it.

Dad watched quietly from the armchair. Sometimes I think he spent all his time just sitting there, thinking. But maybe he didn't really think about anything. Maybe he just closed his eyes and received the present with calm or resignation. That night he spoke, though: "This is a good thing," he told me. "You overcame adversity." Mom looked at him suspiciously, but he went on stringing together a confused speech about adversity.

I lay back on the chair across from him and pretended to fall asleep. I heard them argue, always the same pattern. Mom would say five sentences and Dad would answer with a single word. Sometimes he would answer sharply: "No." Sometimes he would say, practically shouting: "Liar." Sometimes he would even say, like the police: "Negative."

That night Mom carried me to bed and told me, perhaps knowing I was only pretending to sleep and was listening, curious and attentive: "Your father is right. Now we know you won't get lost. That you know how to walk in the street alone. But you should concentrate more on the way. You should walk faster."

I listened to her. From then on, I walked faster. In fact, a couple of years later, the first time I talked to Claudia, she asked me why I walked so fast. She had been following me for days, spying on me. We had met not long before, on March 3, 1985—the night of the earthquake—but we hadn't talked then.

She was twelve and I was nine, so our friendship was impossible. But we were friends, or something like it. We talked a lot. Sometimes I think I'm writing this book just to remember those conversations.

THE NIGHT OF THE EARTHQUAKE I WAS SCARED
but I also, in a way, enjoyed what was happening.

In the front yard of one of the houses, the adults put up two tents for the children to sleep in, and at first it was chaos because we all wanted to sleep in the one that looked like an igloo—those were still a novelty back then—but they gave that one to the girls. So we boys shut ourselves in to fight in silence, which was what we did when we were alone: hit each other furiously, happily. But then the red-head's nose started bleeding, so we had to find another game.

Someone thought of making wills, and at first it seemed like a good idea; after a while, though, we decided it didn't make sense, because if a bigger earthquake came and ended the world, there wouldn't be anyone to leave our things to. Then we imagined that the earth was like a dog shaking itself so people fell off like fleas into space, and we thought about that image so much it made us laugh, and it also made us sleepy.

But I didn't want to sleep. I was tired like never before, but it was a new tiredness that burned my eyes. I decided to stay up all night and I tried to sneak into the igloo to keep talking to the girls, but the policeman's daughter threw me out, saying I wanted to rape them. Back then I didn't know what a rapist was but I still promised I didn't want to rape them, I just wanted to look at them, and she laughed mockingly and replied that that was what rapists always said. I had to stay outside, listening to them pretend that their dolls were the only survivors; they mourned their owners, crying spectacularly when they realized they were dead, although one of them thought it was for the best, since the human race had always seemed repellent to her. Finally, they argued over who would be in charge. The discussion seemed long to me, but it was easily resolved, since there was only one original Barbie among the dolls: she won.

I found a beach chair among the rubble and shyly approached the adults' bonfire. It was strange to see the neighbors all gathered together, maybe for the first time ever. They drowned their fear in cups of wine and long looks of complicity. Someone brought an old wooden table and threw it casually on the fire. "If you want, I'll throw the guitar on, too," said Dad, and everyone laughed, even me, though I was a little disconcerted because Dad didn't usually tell jokes. That's when our neighbor Raúl returned, and Magali and Claudia were with him. "These are my sister and my niece," he said. After the earthquake he had gone to look for them, and now he was coming back, visibly relieved.

RAÚL WAS THE ONLY PERSON IN THE NEIGH-
borhood who lived alone. It was hard for me to understand
how someone could live alone. I thought that being alone
was a kind of punishment or disease.

The morning he arrived with a mattress strapped to
the roof of his old Fiat 500, I asked my mother when the
rest of his family would come; she answered sweetly that
not everyone had family. Then I thought we should help
him, but after a while I caught on, surprised, that my parents weren't interested in helping Raúl; they didn't think it
was necessary and they even felt a certain reluctance toward that young, thin man. We were neighbors, we shared
a wall and a privet hedge, but there was an enormous distance separating us.

It was said around the neighborhood that Raúl was a
Christian Democrat, and that struck me as interesting.
It's hard to explain now why a nine-year-old boy would
be interested that someone was a Christian Democrat.
Maybe I thought there was some connection between
being a Christian Democrat and the sad circumstance of
living alone. I had never seen Dad speak to Raúl, so I was
surprised to see them sharing a few cigarettes that night.
I thought they must be talking about solitude, that Dad
was giving our neighbor advice about how to overcome soli-

tude, though Dad must have known very little about the subject.

Magali, meanwhile, was holding Claudia tightly in a corner, away from the group. The two of them seemed uncomfortable. I remember thinking that they must have been uncomfortable because they were different from the rest of the people gathered there. Politely, but perhaps with a trace of malice, one neighbor asked Magali what she did for a living; Magali answered immediately, as if she'd been expecting the question, that she was an English teacher.

It was very late and I was sent to bed. I had to reluctantly make space for myself in the tent. I was afraid I might fall asleep, but I distracted myself by listening to those stray voices in the night. I understood that Raúl had taken his relatives home, because people started to talk about them. Someone said the girl was strange. She hadn't seemed strange to me. She had seemed beautiful. "And the woman," said my mother, "didn't have an English teacher's face."

"She had the face of a housewife, nothing more," added another neighbor, and they drew out the joke for a while.

I thought about an English teacher's face, about what an English teacher's face should be like. I thought about my mother, my father. I thought: What kinds of faces do my parents have? But our parents never really have faces. We never learn to truly look at them.

I THOUGHT WE WOULD SPEND WEEKS OR EVEN months outside, waiting for some far-off truck to bring supplies and blankets. I even imagined myself talking on TV, thanking my fellow Chileans for their help, the way I'd seen people do during the rainstorms. I thought about the terrible floods of other years, when we couldn't go out and we were practically obligated to sit in front of the screen and watch the people who had lost everything.

But it wasn't like that. Calm returned almost immediately. The worst always happened to other people. In that lost corner west of Santiago the earthquake had been no more than an enormous scare. A few shacks fell down, but there was no great damage and no one died. The TV showed the San Antonio port destroyed, as well as some streets I had seen or thought I had seen on rare trips to downtown Santiago. I confusedly intuited that the true suffering happened there.

If there was anything to learn, we didn't learn it. Now I think it's a good thing to lose confidence in the solidity of the ground, I think it's necessary to know that from one moment to the next everything can come tumbling down. But at the time we went back, just like that, to life as usual.

Once we were back in the house, Dad confirmed that the damage was slight: just some plaster fallen from the walls and a cracked window. Mom mourned only the loss of the zodiac glasses. Eight of them broke, including hers (Pisces), Dad's (Leo), and the one Grandma used when she came to see us (Scorpio).

"No problem, we have other glasses, we don't need any more," said Dad, and she answered without looking at him, looking at me: "Only yours survived." Then she went to get the glass with the Libra sign, and gave it to me with a solemn gesture. She spent the following days a little depressed, contemplating giving the remaining glasses to Geminis, Virgos, Aquarians.

The good news was that we wouldn't go back to school right away. The old building had suffered significant damage, and those who had seen it said it was a pile of rubble. It was hard for me to imagine the school destroyed, though it wasn't sadness that I felt. I just felt curious. I especially remembered the bare spot at the edge of the playground where we went at recess, and the wall the middle school kids would scribble on. I thought about all those messages smashed to smithereens, scattered in the ash on the ground—bawdy sayings, phrases for or against Colo-Colo, or for or against Pinochet. One phrase I found especially funny: *Pinochet sucks dick.*

Back then I was, as I always have been, and I always will be, for Colo-Colo. As for Pinochet, to me he was a television personality who hosted a show with no fixed schedule, and I hated him for that, for the stuffy national channels that interrupted their programming during the best parts. Later I hated him for being a son of a bitch, for being a murderer, but back then I hated him only for those inconvenient shows that Dad watched without saying a word, without acceding any movement other than a more forceful drag on the cigarette he always had glued to his lips.

AROUND THEN, THE REDHEAD'S FATHER TOOK a trip to Miami, and he returned with a baseball glove and bat for his son. The gift brought about an unexpected break in our routine. For many days we switched from soccer to that slow and slightly stupid game which nevertheless entranced my friends. It was absurd: ours must have been the only neighborhood in the country where the kids played baseball instead of soccer. It was hard for me to hit the ball or throw it straight and I was quickly sent to the bench. The redhead, who had been one of my best friends, suddenly became popular. Now he preferred the company of the older kids who were attracted by the foreign game and had joined our group. And that's how, because of baseball, I was left friendless.

In the afternoons, resigned to solitude, I would leave the house, as they say, to tire myself out: I walked in wider and wider circuits, though I almost always respected a certain geometry of circles. I exhausted all possible routes, all the blocks, took in new landscapes, though the world didn't vary too much: the same new houses, built quickly, as if obeying some urgency, but nevertheless solid and re-silient. In a few weeks most of the walls had been restored and reinforced. It was hard to tell there had just been an earthquake.

Now I don't understand that freedom we enjoyed. We lived under a dictatorship; people talked about crimes and attacks, martial law and curfew, but even so, nothing kept me from spending all day wandering far from home. Weren't the streets of Maipú dangerous then? At night they were, and during the day as well, but the adults played, arrogantly or innocently—or with a mixture of arrogance and innocence—at ignoring the danger. They played at thinking that discontent was a thing of the poor and power the domain of the rich, and in those streets no one was poor or rich, at least not yet.

One of those afternoons I saw Raúl's niece again, but I didn't know if I should say hello. I saw her again several times in the following days. I didn't realize that she was actually following me.

"I just like to walk fast," I answered when she finally spoke to me, and then came a long silence that she broke by asking me if I was lost. I answered that no, I knew per-fectly well how to get home. "It was a joke, I want to talk to you, let's meet next Monday at five in the supermarket bakery." She said it like that, in one sentence, and left.

THE NEXT DAY MY PARENTS WOKE ME UP EARLY because we were going to spend the weekend at Lo Ovalle Reservoir. Mom didn't want to go and she dragged out the preparations, confident that lunchtime would come and the plan would have to change. Dad decided, however, that we would have lunch at a restaurant, and we left right away. Back then, it was a real luxury to eat out. I sat in the backseat of the Peugeot thinking about what I would order, and in the end I asked for a steak *a lo pobre*. Dad warned me that it was a big dish and I wouldn't be able to eat it all, but on those rare outings I was free to order whatever I wanted.

Suddenly, that heavy atmosphere prevailed in which the only possible topic of conversation is the lateness of the food. Our order took so long that finally Dad decided we would leave as soon as the food came. I protested, or I wanted to protest, or now I think I should have protested. "If we're going to leave, let's go now," said Mom resignedly, but Dad explained that this way the restaurant owners would lose the food, that it was an act of justice, of revenge.

We continued our journey ill-humored and hungry. I didn't really like going to the reservoir. They wouldn't let me wander very far by myself and I got bored, though I tried to have fun swimming for a while, fleeing from the rats that lived among the rocks, looking at the worms eating the sawdust and the fish dying on land. Dad settled in to fish all day, and Mom spent the day watching him, and I watched Dad fish and Mom watch him and it was hard for me to understand how that was, for them, fun.

Sunday morning I faked a cold because I wanted to sleep a little longer. They went off to the rocks after giving me endless superfluous instructions. A little while later, I got up and turned on the tape player so I could listen to Raphael while I made breakfast. It was a cassette of all his best songs that my mother had recorded from the radio. Unfortunately, my finger slipped and I pressed "REC" for a few seconds. I ruined the tape right in the chorus of the song "Que sabe nadie."

I was desperate. After thinking a bit, I decided the only solution was to sing over the chorus, and I started practicing the lyric, disguising my voice in a way that seemed convincing to me. Finally I decided to record. I listened to the results several times, thinking, somewhat self-indulgently, that it was good enough. I was a little worried, though, about the lack of music during those seconds.

My father would yell at me, but he didn't hit. He never hit me, it wasn't his style; he preferred the grandiloquence of phrases that were impressive at first, because he said them seriously, like an actor in the final episode of a soap opera: "You've disappointed me as a son, I can never forgive you for what you've done, your behavior is unacceptable," et cetera.

Nonetheless I harbored a delusion that someday he would beat me almost to death. I have a persistent childhood memory of an imminent beating that never came. Because of that fear, the return trip was excruciating. As soon as we set off for Santiago, I declared I was tired of Raphael, and that we should listen to Adamo or José Luis Rodríguez.

"I thought you liked Raphael," said Mom.

"Adamo's lyrics are better," I said, but then it was out of my hands—I accidentally opened up a long discussion about whether Adamo was better than Raphael. Even Julio Iglesias was mentioned, which in any case was absurd, since no one in our family liked Julio Iglesias.

To demonstrate Raphael's vocal quality, my father decided to put in the tape, and when "Que sabe nadie" came on I had to improvise a desperate plan B. This consisted of singing very loudly right from the start of the song; I figured that when the chorus came my voice would just sound louder. They yelled at me for singing so loud, but they didn't notice the adulteration in the tape. Once we were home, however, as I was digging a small hole next to the rose garden to bury the tape, they found me. There was nothing I could do but tell them the whole story. They laughed a lot and listened to the tape several times.

That night, though, they came to my room to tell

me I was grounded for a week, and couldn't leave the house.

"Why are you grounding me after you laughed so much?" I asked, angry.

"Because you lied," said my father.

SO I COULDN'T KEEP MY DATE WITH CLAUDIA, but in the end it was better, because when I told her that story she laughed so much I could look at her without anxiety, forgetting, to some extent, the strange bond that was beginning to connect us.

It's hard for me to remember the circumstances in which we saw each other again. According to Claudia, she was the one who sought me out, but I also remember wandering long hours hoping to run into her. However it happened, suddenly we were walking next to each other again, and she asked me to go with her to her house. We took several turns and she even stopped in the middle of a passage and told me we had to turn around, as if she didn't know where she lived.

We arrived, finally, at a neighborhood with only two streets: Neftalí Reyes Basoalto and Lucila Godoy Alcayaga. It sounds like a joke, but it's true. A lot of the streets in Maipú had, and still have, those absurd names: my cousins, for example, lived on First Symphony Way, near

Second and Third Symphony, perpendicular to Concert Street, and close to the passages Opus One, Opus Two, Opus Three, et cetera. Or the very street where I lived, Aladdin, between Odin and Ramayana and parallel to Lemuria; obviously, toward the end of the seventies some people had a lot of fun choosing names for the streets where the new families would later live—the families without history, who were willing or perhaps resigned to live in that fantasy world.

"I live in the neighborhood of real names," said Claudia on the afternoon of our reencounter, looking seriously into my eyes.

"I live in the neighborhood of real names," she said again, as if she needed to start the sentence over in order to go on: "Lucila Godoy Alcayaga is Gabriela Mistral's real name," she explained. "And Neftalí Reyes Basoalto is Pablo Neruda's real name." A long silence came over us, which I broke by saying the first thing that came into my head:

"Living here must be much better than living on Aladdin Street."

As I slowly pronounced that stupid sentence, I could see her pimples, her pink-and-white face, her pointed shoulders, the place where her breasts should be but where for now there was nothing, and her hair, unstylish because it wasn't short, wavy, and brown, but rather long, straight, and black.

WE SPENT A WHILE TALKING NEXT TO THE fence, and then she invited me in. I wasn't expecting that, because back then, no one expected that. Each house was a kind of miniature fortress, an impregnable bastion. I myself wasn't allowed to invite friends over; my mother always said the house was too dirty. It wasn't true, the house sparkled, but I thought that maybe there was some kind of dirt that I simply couldn't see, and that when I grew up maybe I would see layers of dust where now I saw only waxed floors and shining wood.

Claudia's house seemed fairly similar to my own: the same horrible raffia swans, two or three little Mexican hats, several minuscule clay pots and crochet dishcloths. The first thing I did was ask to use the bathroom, and I discovered, astonished, that the house had two bathrooms. Never before had I been in a house that had two bathrooms. My idea of wealth was exactly that: I imagined that millionaires must have houses with three bathrooms, or even five.

Claudia told me she wasn't sure her mother would be happy to see me there, and I asked if it was because of the dust. She didn't understand at first but she listened to my explanation, and then she chose to answer that yes, her mother didn't like her to invite friends over because she thought the house was always dirty. I asked her then, without thinking about it too much, about her father.

"My father doesn't live with us," she said. "My parents are separated, he lives in another city." I asked her if she missed him. "Of course I do. He's my father."

In my class there was only one boy with separated parents, which to me was a stigma, the saddest situation imaginable.

"Maybe they'll live together again someday," I said, to console her.

"Maybe," she said. "But I don't feel like talking about that. I want us to talk about something else."

She took off her sandals, went to the kitchen, and came back with a bowl filled with bunches of black, green, and purple grapes; this struck me as odd, because in my house we never bought such a variety of grapes. I took advantage of the chance to try them all, and while I compared the flavors, Claudia filled the silence with general, polite questions. "I need to ask you something," she said finally, "but not till after lunch."

"If you want, I'll help you fix the food," I said, though I had never cooked in my life, or helped anyone else cook.

"We're already having lunch," said Claudia, very seriously. "These grapes are lunch."

It was hard for her to get to the point. She seemed to speak freely, but there was also a stutter to her words that made it difficult to understand her. Really, she wanted to keep quiet. Now I think she was cursing the fact that she had to talk in order for me to understand what she wanted to ask me.

ʻI NEED YOU TO TAKE CARE OF HIM,ʼ SHE SAID suddenly, forgetting all her strategy.

"Who?"

"My uncle. I need you to take care of him."

"Okay," I answered immediately, so reliable, and in a split second I imagined that Raúl was suffering from some horrible disease, a disease maybe even worse than solitude, and that I would have to be some kind of nurse. I imagined myself walking around the neighborhood, pushing him in his wheelchair and blessed for my selflessness. But evidently that wasn't what Claudia was asking me for. She spilled out the story all at once, looking at me fixedly, and I agreed quickly but at the wrong time—I agreed too quickly, as if confident that I would figure out later on what Claudia had really asked of me.

What I eventually understood was that Claudia and her mother couldn't or shouldn't visit Raúl, at least not often. That's where I came in: I had to watch over Raúl; not take care of him but rather keep an eye on his activities and make notes about anything that seemed suspicious. We would meet every Thursday, at the random meeting point she had chosen, the supermarket bakery, where I would give her my report and then we would talk for a while about other things. "Because," she told me, "I'm really interested in how you're doing." And I smiled with a satisfaction in which fear and desire also breathed.

I STARTED SPYING ON RAÚL RIGHT AWAY. THE job was boring and easy, or maybe it was difficult, because I was searching blindly. From my conversations with Claudia I was vaguely expecting to see silent men with dark sunglasses traveling at midnight in foreign cars, but nothing like that went on at Raúl's house. His routine hadn't changed: he went out and came back at regular office hours, and he greeted people he met with a stiff and friendly nod that precluded all possibility of conversation. In any case, I didn't want to talk to him. I was just waiting for him to do something unusual, something that was worth telling his niece.

I arrived on time or early to my meetings with Claudia, but she was always already there, in front of the pastry case. It was as if she spent the entire day looking at those pastries. She seemed worried about our being seen together, and every time we met she pretended it was coincidental. We walked around the supermarket, peering attentively at the products as if we really were out shopping; we left with nothing but a couple of yogurts that we opened at the end of a zigzagging route that began in the plaza and followed side streets to the Maipú Temple. Only when we sat down on the temple's long steps did she feel safe. The faithful few who appeared at that hour passed by with lowered gazes, as if getting a head start on their prayers or confessions.

More than once I wanted to know why we had to hide, and Claudia would only say that we had to be careful, that everything could be ruined. Of course, I didn't know what it was that could be ruined, but by that point I'd already gotten used to her vague answers.

However, on a whim one afternoon I told her that I knew the truth: I knew that Raúl's problems had to do with the fact that he was a Christian Democrat, and she burst out in a long, excessive peal of laughter. She seemed to regret it immediately. She came over, put her hands ceremoniously on my shoulders, and I even thought she was going to kiss me; but that wasn't it, of course.

"My uncle isn't a Christian Democrat," she told me in a calm and slow voice.

Then I asked her if he was a Communist and she fell into a heavy silence.

"I can't tell you any more," she answered finally. "It's not important. You don't need to know everything in order to do your job." She decided, suddenly, to follow that train of thought, and she talked quickly and a lot: she said she would understand if I didn't want to help her, and maybe it would be better for us to stop seeing each other. When I pleaded for our meetings to continue, she asked me to just concentrate on watching Raúl in the future.

TO ME, A COMMUNIST WAS SOMEONE WHO read the newspaper and silently bore the mockery of others—I thought of my grandfather, my father's father, who was always reading the newspaper. Once I asked him if he read the whole thing, and the old man answered that yes, when it came to the newspaper you had to read it all.

I also had a memory of a violent scene, a conversation at my grandparents' house during independence week. They and their five children were sitting around the main table and I was with my cousins at what they called the kids' table, when my father said to my grandfather at the end of an argument, almost shouting: "Shut up, you old Communist!" At first everyone was quiet, but little by little they started laughing. Even my grandmother and my mother laughed, and even one of my cousins, who certainly didn't understand the situation. They didn't just laugh, they also repeated it, openly mocking: you old Communist.

I thought my grandfather would laugh too, that it was one of those liberating moments when everyone gives themselves over to laughter. But the old man stayed very serious, in silence. He didn't say a word. They treated him badly and back then I wasn't sure he deserved it.

Years later I learned he hadn't been a good father. He wasted his life gambling away his laborer's salary, and he lived off his wife, who sold vegetables and washed clothes and sewed. Growing up, it was my father's duty to go around to the dive bars looking for him, asking for him, knowing that in the best of cases he would find him hugging the dregs of a bottle.

CLASSES STARTED UP AGAIN AND THEY RE-placed our head teacher, Miss Carmen, which I was grateful for with all my heart. She had been our teacher for three years, and now I think she wasn't a bad person, but she hated me. She hated me because of the word *aguja*, which for her didn't exist. For her, the correct word was *ahuja*. I don't know why one day I decided to take the dictionary up to her and show her she had it wrong. She looked at me in panic, swallowing saliva, and she nodded, but from then on she no longer liked me nor I her. We shouldn't hate the person who teaches us, for better or for worse, to read. But I hated her, or rather I hated the fact that she hated me.

Mr. Morales, on the other hand, liked me from the

start, and I trusted him enough to ask him one morning, while we were walking to the gym for P.E. class, if it was very bad to be a Communist.

"Why do you ask that?" he said. "Do you think I'm a Communist?"

"No," I said. "I'm sure you're not a Communist."

"And are you a Communist?"

"I'm a kid," I told him.

"But if your father was a Communist, you might be one, too."

"I don't think so, because my grandfather is a Communist and my father isn't."

"And what is your father?"

"My father isn't anything," I answered, with certainty.

"It's not good for you to talk about these things," he told me, after looking at me for a long time. "The only thing I can tell you is that we live at a time when it isn't good to talk about these things. But one day we'll be able to talk about this, and about everything else."

"When the dictatorship ends," I told him, as if completing a sentence on a reading test.

He looked at me, laughing, and affectionately patted my hair. "Let's start with ten laps around the field," he shouted, and I started trotting slowly as I thought confusedly about Raúl.

SINCE WE HAD TO MAKE UP THE DAYS WE HAD lost to the earthquake, the school day was extremely long. I got home only half an hour before Raúl, which made my espionage dangerously useless. I decided I had to go deeper, I had to take decisive action, do my job better.

One night, I was walking along the top of the brick wall and I fell into the bushes. I fell hard. Raúl came out right away, very frightened. When he saw me he helped me up and told me I shouldn't be doing that, but that he understood, it was his own fault. I tensed up, not knowing what he was talking about, but then he came back with a tennis ball. "If I'd known it was yours I would have thrown it over into the yard," he said, and I thanked him.

A little later I heard, clearly, Raúl's voice talking to another man. Their voices sounded close by, they had to be in the room contiguous to my bedroom. I'd never heard any sounds coming from that room before, although I was in the habit of putting my ear to a glass against the wall and listening. I couldn't make out what they were talking about. I did notice that they talked very little. It was not a fluid conversation. It was the kind of conversation that happens between people who know each other well or very little. People who are used to living together, or who don't know each other at all.

The next morning I got up at five thirty and patiently waited until I could find out if the man was still there. Raúl's Fiat 500 left at the same time as always. I hung recklessly out the window and saw that he was alone. I faked a stomachache and my parents let me stay home. I listened silently for a couple of hours until I heard the pipes. The man had to be in the shower. I decided to take a risk. I got dressed, threw the ball at Raúl's house, and rang the bell several times, but the man didn't come out. I waited without ringing again. I saw him leave the house and walk down Odin, so I ran along Aladdin to circle the block and meet him head-on. I stopped him and told him I was lost, and asked if he could please help me get home again.

The man looked at me with barely concealed annoyance, but he went with me. When we arrived he didn't mention that he had spent the night at Raúl's house. I thanked him and then I had no other option: I asked him if he knew Raúl, and he answered that they were cousins, that he lived in Puerto Montt, and that he had stayed at Raúl's house because he had an errand to run in Santiago.

"I'm Raúl's neighbor," I told him.

"See you later, Raúl's neighbor," said the man, and he set off quickly, almost running.

`IT'S POSSIBLE,' SAID CLAUDIA, TO MY SUR-
prise, when I told her about the stranger. It was possible
that Raúl had a cousin in Puerto Montt? Wouldn't that
cousin, then, be related to Claudia?

"We have a very big family," said Claudia, "and there
are a lot of uncles in the south I've never met." She serenely
changed the subject.

There were five other men at Raúl's house in the following
months, and each time Claudia seemed unaffected by the
news. But she had a very different reaction when I told her
that a woman had stayed there, and not for one night, as
usual, but for two nights in a row.

"Maybe she came from the south, too," I said.

"Could be," she answered, but she was obviously surprised, even angry.

"She could be a girlfriend. Maybe Raúl isn't alone anymore," I said.

"Yes," she answered, after a while. "Raúl is single, it's
entirely possible he could have a girlfriend. In any case, I
want you to find out everything you can about that possible girlfriend."

She seemed to be struggling not to cry. I looked at her
closely until she stood up. "Let's go inside the temple," she

28

said. She dipped her fingers into the bowl of holy water and used it to cool her face. We stayed on our feet next to some enormous candelabra with wax dripping from the candles—some new and others about to burn out—that people would bring when they prayed for miracles. Claudia put her hands over the flames as if to warm them; she dipped her fingertips in the wax, and played at making the sign of the cross with her wax-coated fingers. She didn't know the sign of the cross. I taught her.

We sat in the first pew. I looked obediently at the altar, while Claudia looked to the sides and identified, one by one, the flags that flanked the statue of the virgin. She asked me if I knew why the flags were there. "They're the flags of the Americas," I said.

"Yes, but why are they here?"

"I don't know," I answered. "Something about the unity of the Americans, I guess."

She took my hand and told me that the prettiest flag was Argentina's. "Which one do you think is prettiest?" she asked me, and I was going to say the United States flag but luckily I kept quiet, because then she said the United States flag was the ugliest, a truly horrible flag, and I added that I agreed, the United States flag was really disgusting.

FOR WEEKS I WAITED FRUITLESSLY FOR THE woman to return. Then she appeared, finally, one Saturday morning. She was a girl, really. I figured she was around eighteen years old. She could hardly have been Raúl's girl-friend.

I spent hours trying to hear what she and Raúl talked about, but they exchanged barely a few sentences that I couldn't understand. I thought she would spend the night, but she left that same afternoon. I followed her, absurdly camouflaged by a red cap. The woman walked quickly to-ward a bus stop and when I got there, next to her, I wanted to say something but my voice wouldn't come.

The bus pulled up and I had to decide, in a matter of sec-onds, whether I would follow her onto it. At that time I al-ready rode the bus alone, but only on the short, ten-minute ride to school. I got on and rode for a long time, a bold hour-and-a-half foray I spent rooted to the seat right behind hers.

I had never traveled so far from home on my own, and the powerful impression the city left on me is, in some way, the one that still rears up now and then: a formless space, open but also closed, with imprecise plazas that are almost always empty, and people walking along narrow sidewalks, gazing at the ground with a kind of deaf fervor, as if they could only move forward along a forced anonymity.

Night fell over that forbidden neck as I looked at it ever more fixedly, as if staring would free me from that flight, as if watching her intensely would protect me. By that point the bus was starting to fill up and one woman looked at me, expecting me to give her my seat, but I couldn't risk losing my place. I decided to act like I was mentally retarded, or the way I thought a mentally retarded boy would act—a boy who looked straight ahead, entranced and completely absorbed by an imaginary world.

Raúl's supposed girlfriend got off the bus suddenly and almost left me behind. I barely made it to the door, elbowing my way out. She waited for me and helped me down. I kept moving like a retarded child, though she knew full well that I wasn't a retarded child but rather Raúl's neighbor who had followed her, who seemed resolved to follow her all night long. There was no reproach in her gaze, though—only an absolute serenity.

I ventured with pointless discretion into a maze of streets that seemed big and old. Every once in a while she would turn around, smile at me, and speed up, as if it were a game and not an extremely serious matter. Suddenly she started to trot and then took off running, just like that, and I almost lost her; then I saw her go into a shop far ahead. I climbed a tree and waited several minutes for her to finally come out, assuming I would be gone. Then she walked just half a block farther, to what had to be her house. I waited until she had gone in and I went closer. The fence was green and the facade was blue, and that caught my attention, because I had never seen that color combination before. I wrote the address in my notebook, happy to have gotten such exact information.

I had a hard time getting back to the street where I had to catch the return bus. But I remembered the name clearly: Tobalaba. I got home at one in the morning, and I was so frightened that I couldn't even outline a convincing explanation. My parents had gone to the police, and the affair had leaked to the neighbors. I finally told them I had fallen asleep in a plaza and had only just woken up. They believed me, and later they even made me see a doctor who checked me for sleep disorders.

Emboldened by my discoveries, I arrived at our Thursday date firmly intending to tell Claudia everything I knew about Raúl's supposed girlfriend.

BUT THINGS DIDN'T TURN OUT THAT WAY. Claudia arrived late to the meeting, and she wasn't alone. With a friendly gesture she introduced me to Esteban, a guy with long blond hair. She told me I could trust him and that he knew the whole story. I tensed up, disconcerted, not daring to ask if he was her boyfriend or cousin or what. He must have been seventeen or eighteen years old: a little older than Claudia, a lot older than me.

Esteban bought three *marraquetas* and a quarter of a

kilo of mortadella at the supermarket. We didn't go to the temple. We stayed in the plaza to eat. The guy didn't talk much, but that afternoon I spoke even less. I didn't tell Claudia what I had discovered, maybe as a form of revenge, since I wasn't prepared for what was happening; I couldn't understand why someone else was allowed to know what I was doing with Claudia, why she was allowed to share our secret.

I acted like the child I was and missed our meetings after that. I thought that was what I should do: forget about Claudia. But after a few weeks I was surprised to get a letter from her. She summoned me urgently, asking me to come see her anytime; she said it didn't matter if her mother was home or not.

It was almost nine at night. Magali opened the door and asked my name, but it was obvious she already knew it. Claudia greeted me effusively and told her mother that I was Raúl's neighbor, and Magali made excessive gestures of delight. "You've grown so much," she said, "I didn't recognize you." I'm sure they were performing a rehearsed introduction, and the questions the woman directed at me were entirely studied in advance. A bit bewildered by the situation, I asked if she was still an English teacher, and she answered with a smile that yes, it wasn't easy to stop, overnight, being an English teacher.

I asked Claudia to tell me what had happened: How had things changed so much that now my presence was legitimate?

"It's more like things are changing little by little," she told me. "Very slowly, things are changing. You don't need to spy on Raúl anymore, you can come and see me whenever you want, but you don't have to make any reports," she repeated, and all I could do was leave, brooding over a deep disquiet.

I WENT TO CLAUDIA'S ONE OR TWO MORE times, but I ran into Esteban again. I never found out if he was her boyfriend or not, but in any case I detested him. And then I stopped going, and the days went by like a gust of wind. For some months or maybe a year I forgot all about Claudia. Until one morning I saw Raúl loading up a white truck with dozens of boxes.

Everything happened very quickly. I went up to him and asked where he was going, and he didn't answer: he looked at me with a neutral and evasive gesture. I took off running to Claudia's house. I wanted to warn her, and as I was running I discovered that I also wanted her to forgive me. But Claudia wasn't there anymore.

"They left a few days ago," said the woman next door. "I don't know where they went, how should I know that?" she said. "To another neighborhood, I guess."

LITERATURE OF THE
PARENTS

I'M ADVANCING LITTLE BY LITTLE IN THE novel. I pass the time thinking about Claudia as if she existed, as if she had existed. At first I questioned even her name. But it's the name 90 percent of the women of my generation share. It's right that she should have that name. I never get tired of the sound, either. Claudia.

I like that my characters don't have last names. It's a relief.

»»»«««

One of these days this house will start to refuse me. I wanted to start to inhabit it again, organize the books, rearrange the furniture, fix up the yard a bit. None of that has possible. But a few fingers of mescal are helping for now.

This afternoon I spoke, for the second time in a long time, with Eme. We asked about the friends we have in common, and then, after more than a year of separation, we talked about the books she took with her or accidentally forgot. It seemed painful to go over the list of losses in such a civilized way, but in the end I even roused myself to ask for the books by Hebe Uhart and Josefina Vicens that I've missed so much.

"I read them," she said. For a second I thought she was lying, even though she never lies about things like that; she never lied about anything, really. That was exactly our problem, we didn't lie. We failed because of the desire to always be honest.

Then she told me about the house where she lives—a mansion, really, some twenty blocks from here, which she shares with two girlfriends.

"You don't know them," she told me, "and they aren't really my friends, but we make a good group: thirty-year-old women happily chatting about our frustrations." I told her I could go see her and bring the books she needed. She said no. "I want to come over myself, one of these days, after Christmas. You can give me a cup of tea and we'll talk," she said.

"Since we've been separated," she added suddenly, forcing or searching for a natural tone, "since we've been separated I've slept with two men."

"I haven't been with any," I answered, joking.

"Then you haven't changed all that much," she told me, laughing.

"But I've been with two women," I told her. The truth is that it's been only one. I lied, maybe to even the score.

Still, I couldn't go on with the game. "The mere idea of you with someone else is unbearable," I said, and we had a hard time, after that, filling the silence.

I remember the day she left. It's supposed to be the man who leaves the house. While she cried and packed her things, the only thing I managed to say to her was that absurd sentence: "It's supposed to be the man who leaves the house." In some ways I still feel that this space is hers. That's why it's so hard for me to live here.

Talking to her again was good and perhaps necessary. I told her about the new novel. I said that at first I was keeping a steady pace, but little by little I had lost the rhythm, or the precision.

"Why don't you just write it all at once?" she advised, as if she didn't know me, as if she hadn't been with me through so many nights of writing.

"I don't know," I answered. And it's true, I don't know.

The thing is, Eme—I think now, a little drunk—I'm waiting for a voice. A voice that isn't mine. An old voice, novelistic and solid.

Or maybe it's just that I like working on the book. That I prefer writing to having written. I'd rather stay there, inhabit the time of the book, cohabit with those years, chase the distant images at length and then carefully go over them again. See them badly, but see them. To just stay there, looking.

As is to be expected, I spent the whole day thinking about Eme. It's thanks to her that I found the story for the novel. It must have been five years ago, when we had just moved into this house. We were still in bed at noon and were telling anecdotes from our childhoods, as lovers do who want to know everything, who cast about for old stories to exchange with the other person, who also searches: to find themselves in that illusion of control, of surrender.

She was seven or eight years old, in the yard with other little girls, playing hide-and-seek. It was getting late, time to go inside; the adults were calling and the girls answered that they were coming. The push and pull went on, the calls were more and more urgent, but the girls laughed and kept playing.

Suddenly they realized the adults had stopped calling them a while ago and night had already fallen. They thought the adults must be watching them, trying to teach them a lesson, and that now the grown-ups were the ones playing hide-and-seek. But no. When she went inside, Eme saw that her father's friends were crying and that her mother, rooted to her seat, was staring off into space. They were listening to the news on the radio. A voice was talking about a raid. It talked about the dead, about more dead.

"That happened so many times," Eme said that day, five years ago. "We kids understood, all of a sudden, that we weren't so important. That there were unfathomable and serious things that we couldn't know or understand."

The novel belongs to our parents, I thought then, I

think now. That's what we grew up believing, that the novel belonged to our parents. We cursed them, and also took refuge in their shadows, relieved. While the adults killed or were killed, we drew pictures in a corner. While the country was falling to pieces, we were learning to talk, to walk, to fold napkins in the shape of boats, of airplanes. While the novel was happening, we played hide-and-seek, we played at disappearing.

>>>«««

Instead of writing, I spent the morning drinking beer and reading *Madame Bovary*. Now I think the best thing I've done in recent years has been to drink a lot of beer and reread certain books with dedication, with an odd fidelity, as if something of my own beat within them, some clue to my destiny. Apart from that, to read morosely, stretched out in bed for long hours and doing nothing to soothe my burning eyes—it's the perfect pretext for waiting for night to fall. And that's what I hope for, nothing more: that night will come quickly.

I still remember the afternoon when the teacher turned to the blackboard and wrote the words *quiz*, *next*, *Friday*, *Madame*, *Bovary*, *Gustave*, *Flaubert*, *French*. With each letter the silence grew, until finally only the sad squeak of the chalk could be heard.

By that time we had already read long novels, some almost as long as *Madame Bovary*, but this time the deadline was impossible: we had less than a week to confront a four-hundred-page novel. We were starting to get used to those surprises, though: we had just entered the National Institute, we were eleven or twelve years old, and we understood that from then on, all the books would be long.

I feel sure that those teachers didn't want to inspire enthusiasm for books, but rather to deter us from them, to put us off books forever. They didn't waste their spit talking about the joy of reading, maybe because they had lost that joy or they'd never really felt it. Supposedly they were good teachers, but back then being good meant little more than knowing the textbook.

After a while we learned the tricks that were passed down from one generation to the next. They taught us to be cheaters, and we were fast learners. Every test had a section of character identification, which included only secondary characters: the less relevant the characters, the more likely we would be asked about them, so we memorized names resignedly, though with the pleasure of guaranteed points. It was important to know that the errand boy with a limp was named Hipólito and the maid was Félicité, and that the name of Emma's daughter was Berta Bovary.

There was a certain beauty in the act, because back then we were exactly that: secondary characters, hundreds of children who crisscrossed the city lugging denim backpacks. The neighbors would test the weight and always make the same joke: "What are you carrying in there, rocks?" Downtown Santiago welcomed us with tear gas bombs, but we weren't carrying rocks, we were carrying bricks by Baldor or Villee or Flaubert.

Madame Bovary was one of the few novels we had in our house, so I started reading that very same night, but I grew impatient with all the description. Flaubert's prose simply made me doze off. I had to resort to the emergency method my father taught me: read the first two pages and then the last two, and only then, only after knowing how the novel begins and ends, do you continue reading in order.

"Even if you don't finish, at least you already know who the killer is," said my father, who apparently only read books that had killers.

So the first thing I ascertained about *Madame Bovary* was that the shy, tall boy from the first chapter would ultimately die, and that his daughter would end up as a laborer in a cotton factory. I already knew about Emma's suicide, since some of the parents had complained that suicide was too harsh a subject for children of twelve, to which the teacher replied that no, the suicide of a woman hounded by debt was a very contemporary subject, one that children of twelve could understand perfectly well.

I didn't get much further in my reading. I studied the summaries my deskmate had written, and the day before the test I found a copy of the movie in the Maipú video store. My mother tried to keep me from watching it, saying it wasn't appropriate for my age; I thought so too—or rather, I hoped so. *Madame Bovary* sounded pornographic to me; everything French sounded pornographic to me.

In that sense, the movie was a disappointment, but I watched it twice and filled in the required worksheets on both sides. I got only a 3.6 after all that, and for some time I associated *Madame Bovary* with a 3.6, which I also tied to the name of the film's director, written with exclamation points by my teacher next to my bad grade: Vincente Minnelli!!

Now I look for Berta in the novel. I remembered only the moment, in Chapter Five of the second part, when Emma looks at Berta and thinks, surprised, Look how ugly the girl is. And the terrible scene of Charles's death, when Berta thinks her father is pretending: "Thinking he was playing a joke on her, she gave him a little push. Bovary fell to the floor. He was dead."

I like to imagine Berta prowling about the yard while her mother is in bed, convalescing: from her room, Emma hears the sound of a carriage, and she approaches the window with difficulty to look down at the now deserted street.

I like to imagine Berta learning to read. First, Emma is the one who tries to teach her. After her great disappointment, she has decided to rededicate her life and become a woman of pious occupations. Berta is still very small and surely doesn't understand the lessons. But during those days or weeks or months her mother has all the patience in the world: she teaches her daughter to read and mends clothes for the poor and even reads religious books.

Sometime later, Charles takes Berta on a walk and tries to teach her to read using a medical book. But the girl isn't in the habit of studying, so she gets sad and starts to cry.

There's a passage where Charles thinks about Berta's future, and of course he is very wrong when he imagines her at fifteen, strolling in the summertime wearing a big straw hat, as beautiful as her mother. "Looking at them from far away they look like sisters," thinks Charles, satisfied.

»»«««

Eme finally came over. As a Christmas gift she gave me a box of magnets with hundreds of English words. We assembled the first phrase together, which turned out, somehow, to be opportune:

only love & noise

She showed me her recent drawings, but wouldn't read the first pages of my book. She looked at me with a new expression, one I didn't recognize.

It's amazing: the face of a loved one, the face of someone we've lived with, whom we think we know, maybe the only face we would be able to describe, which we've looked at for years, from up close—it's beautiful and in a certain way terrible to know that even that face can suddenly, unpredictably, unleash new expressions. Expressions we've never seen before. Expressions that perhaps we'll never see again.

>>>«««

Back then we didn't know the names of the streets, of the trees, of the birds. We didn't need to. We lived with few words and it was possible to answer any question by saying: I don't know. We didn't think it was ignorance. We called it honesty. Later we learned, little by little, the nuances. The names of trees, birds, rivers. And we decided that any words were better than silence.

But I'm against nostalgia.

No, that's not true. I'd like to be against nostalgia. Everywhere you look there's someone renewing vows with the past. We recall songs we never really liked, we meet up with our first girlfriends again, or classmates we didn't get along with, we greet with open arms people we used to reject.

I'm amazed at the ease with which we forget what we felt, what we wanted. The speed with which we assume that now we want or feel something different. And at the same time we want to laugh at the same jokes. We want to be, we believe we are again, children who are blessed by shadow.

I'm in that trap now, in the novel. Yesterday I wrote the reunion scene that takes place almost twenty years later. I liked how it turned out, but sometimes I think the characters shouldn't meet again. That perhaps they should pass each other by many times, walk down the same streets, maybe even talk to each other without recognizing each other, from one side of a counter to the other.

Do we really recognize someone twenty years later? Can we recognize now, in some luminous sign, the definitive features, irrevocably adult, of a bygone face? I've spent the afternoon thinking about that, deliberating that.

It seems beautiful to me for them to never reunite. To simply go on with separate lives until the present, slowly getting closer and closer: two parallel trajectories that never quite meet. But someone else will have to write that novel. I would like to read it. Because in the novel I want to write they meet again. I need for them to meet again.

>>»«<<

"Do they fall in love? Is it a love story?"

Eme asks this and I just smile. She arrived mid-afternoon; we drank several cups of tea and listened to an entire Kinks album. I asked her to let me read her a few pages of the manuscript and again she refused. "I'd rather read them when you're further along," she said.

"I'm writing about you, the protagonist is a lot like you," I said bravely.

"All the more reason," she answered, smiling, "I'd rather read it when you're further along. But I'm so happy you've started writing again," she added. "I like what happens to you when you write. Writing is good for you, it protects you."

"Protects me from what?"

"The words protect you. You search for phrases, you search for words, that's really good," she said.

Later she asked me for more details about the story. I told her very little, the minimum. When I talked about Claudia, I started to question her name again.

She asked me later, half-joking, if the characters stay together for the rest of their lives. I couldn't avoid a flicker of annoyance. I answered no: they see each other again as adults and they get involved for a few weeks, maybe months, but in no way do they stay together. I told her it couldn't be like that, it's never like that.

"It's never like that in good novels, but in bad novels anything is possible," said Eme as she tied up her hair nervously, flirtatiously.

I looked at her chapped lips, her cheeks, her short eyelashes. She seemed to be sunk into a deep contemplation. Soon after, she left. I didn't want her to leave yet. But she left. She's taking serious precautions. I agree, I don't think it would be good for us to live together again either, for now. We need time.

Afterward I tried to keep writing. I don't know which direction to take. I don't want to talk about innocence or guilt; I want nothing more than to illuminate some corners, the corners where we were. But I'm not sure I can do it well. I feel too close to what I'm telling. I've abused some memories, I've sacked my memory, and also, in a certain way, I've made up too much. I'm starting from scratch again, like a caricature of a writer staring impotently at the screen.

I didn't tell Eme how hard it is for me to write without her. I remember her sleepy face, when I went to her very late to read her just a paragraph or a sentence. She listened and nodded or else said, accurately: It wouldn't be like that, this character wouldn't answer with those words. Those kinds of valuable, essential observations.

Now I'm going to write again with her, I think. And I feel happy.

»»»«««

Last night I walked for hours. It was as if I wanted to get lost down some unknown street. To get absolutely and happily lost. But there are moments when we can't, when we don't know how to lose our way. Even if we always go in the wrong direction. Even if we lose all our points of reference. Even if it begins to grow late and we feel the weight of morning as we advance. There are times when no matter how we try to find out what we don't know, we can't lose our way. And perhaps we long for the time when we could be lost. The time when all the streets were new.

I've spent several days remembering the landscape of Maipú, comparing its image—a world of identical houses, red bricks and vinyl flooring—with the old streets where I've lived for years now, where each house is different from the next—uneven bricks, parquet floors—these noble streets that don't belong to me but that I travel with familiarity. Streets named after people, after real places, after battles lost and won, and not those fantastical streets, that false world where we grew up quickly.

>>»«<<

This morning I saw a woman reading, on a bench in Inter-communal Park. I sat down across from her just to get a look at her face, but it was impossible. The book absorbed her gaze completely, and there were a few moments I believed she was aware of it. That holding the book like that—at the exact height of her eyes, with both hands, her elbows resting on an imaginary table—was her way of hiding.

I saw her white forehead and her almost blond hair, but never her eyes. The book was her disguise, a precious mask.

Her long fingers held up the book like strong, slender branches. I got close enough at one point to see that her nails were ragged, as if she had been chewing them.

I'm sure she sensed my presence, but she didn't lower the book. She held it as if she were meeting someone else's gaze.

To read is to cover one's face, I thought.

To read is to cover one's face. And to write is to show it.

>>»«<<

Today I watched *The Battle of Chile*, the documentary by Patricio Guzmán. I'd only seen bits and pieces, mostly from the second part of the film when they showed it once at school, after democracy was restored. I remember how the student president narrated the scenes, and every so often would stop the tape so he could tell us how seeing these images was more important than learning the multiplication tables.

We understood, of course, what he was trying to say, but his example still seemed strange to us, because if we were in that school it was precisely because we had known the multiplication tables for many years. Someone in the last row of the auditorium interrupted to ask if seeing those images was more important than learning to divide decimals, and then someone asked if, instead of learning the periodic table, we could watch those images over and over, since they were so important. No one laughed, though. The student president didn't want to answer, but he looked at us with a mixture of sadness and irony. Then another representative intervened and said: "There are some things you shouldn't joke about. If you understand that, you can stay in the room."

I didn't remember or I hadn't seen the long sequence of *The Battle of Chile* that takes place in the fields of Maipú. Workers and peasants defend the land and argue heatedly with a representative from Salvador Allende's government. I thought how that land could very well be Aladdin Street. The land where, later on, neighborhoods with fantasy names would appear and where we would live, the new families—with no history—of Pinochet's Chile.

School changed a lot when democracy returned. I had just turned thirteen and was belatedly starting to get to know my classmates: children of murdered, tortured, disappeared parents. Children of murderers as well. Rich kids, poor kids, good kids, bad kids. Good rich kids, bad rich kids, good poor kids, bad poor kids. It's absurd to put it that way, but I remember thinking about it more or less like that. I remember thinking, without pride or self-pity, that I was not rich or poor, that I wasn't good or bad. But that was difficult: to be neither good nor bad. It seemed to me, in the end, the same as being bad.

I remember a history teacher I had in high school, when I was sixteen, one whom I didn't particularly like. One morning three thieves who were fleeing the police took cover in the school's parking lot, and the cops followed them and fired a couple of shots into the air. We got scared and threw ourselves to the floor, but once the danger had passed we were surprised to see our teacher crying under the table, with his eyes squeezed shut and his hands over his ears. We brought water and tried to convince him to drink it, but finally we had to throw it in his face. He slowly managed to calm down as we explained to him that no, the military had not taken over again. That class could continue. "I don't want to be here, I never wanted to be here," the teacher repeated, shouting. Then there was complete, compassionate silence. A beautiful and restorative silence.

I ran into the teacher a few days later, during break. I

asked him how he was, and he thanked me for asking. "I can tell you know what I lived through," he said in a sign of complicity. Of course I knew, we all knew; he had been tortured and his cousin was taken prisoner and disappeared. "I don't believe in this democracy," he said. "Chile is and will always be a battleground." He asked me if I was politically active, and I said no. He asked about my family, and I told him that during the dictatorship my parents had kept to the sidelines. The teacher looked at me curiously or disdainfully—he looked at me curiously but I felt that his gaze also held disdain.

>>><<<

I didn't write or read anything in Punta Arenas. I spent the entire week defending myself from the weather and talking with new friends. On the return flight I sat next to two women who told me their life stories in detail. All was well until they asked me what I did for a living. I never know how to respond. I used to say I was a teacher, which tended to lead to long and confused conversations about Chile's crisis in education. So now I say I'm a writer, and when they ask what kind of books I write, I say, to avoid a long and uncertain explanation, that I write action novels; it isn't exactly a lie, since in all novels, even mine, things happen.

Instead of asking what kind of books I write, though, the woman next to me wanted to know what my pseudonym was. I answered that I didn't use a pseudonym. That writers hadn't been using pseudonyms for years now. She looked at me skeptically, and from that moment on her interest in me waned. When we said goodbye she told me not to worry, maybe soon I would come up with a good pseudonym.

>>»>«««

A while ago the poet Rodrigo Olavarría stopped by to see me. We don't know each other well but there is a sort of prior and reciprocal trust that allies us. I like that he gives advice. Now that I think about it, there was a time when everyone gave advice. When life consisted of giving and receiving advice. But then all of a sudden, no one wanted any more advice. It was too late, we'd fallen in love with failure, and the wounds were trophies just like when we were kids, after we'd been playing under the trees. But Rodrigo gives advice. And he listens to it, asks for it. He's in love with failure, but he's also, still, in love with old and noble kinds of friendship.

We spent the afternoon listening to Bill Callahan and Emmy the Great. It was fun. Later I told him about the conversation in the airplane. We decided to get together, one of these days, to choose pseudonyms. "You'll see, we're going to find some great ones," he said.

Rodrigo doesn't remember exactly when he saw *The Battle of Chile* for the first time, but he knows the documentary by heart, because back in Puerto Montt in the mid-eighties his parents sold pirated copies to raise money for the Communist Party's activities. When he was eight or nine, Rodrigo had the job of changing the tapes and stockpiling the new copies in a cardboard box. "I spent the whole afternoon," he told me, "doing homework and copying that documentary two at a time, with four VHS tapes and two TVs. The only breaks were to watch *Robotech* on Channel Thirteen."

»»»«««

Sick with a bad cold, in bed for days. I self-medicate with high doses of television. Eme's visits always seem too short. I asked her again to listen to the first pages of the novel and she again said no. Her excuse was poor and realistic: "You're sick," she said. A little while ago I insisted and she refused again. It's obvious that she doesn't want to read them; maybe she'd rather not resume that part of our relationship.

Well. I just watched *Good Morning*, Ozu's beautiful movie. What greater happiness than to know that movie exists, that I can watch it many times, that I can watch it always.

»»»«««

In the morning I gave myself the stupid task of hiding my cigarettes in different corners of the house. Of course I find them, but I don't smoke much, I smoke less, I struggle to get better once and for all. My illness lasts too long, though, and every once in a while I wonder if I've caught the swine flu. Only the fever is missing, although I've just read on the Internet that some patients don't list fever among their symptoms.

Last night, the emergency room of the Indisa Clinic was full of people with real or imaginary illnesses, but they astonishingly attended to me immediately. There was an explanation. A young, gray-haired doctor appeared and told me, indicating the name tag on his coat: "We're family." And it really is likely that we are related in some way. "I bought your books," he told me, "but I haven't read them." He apologized in a humiliating or merely comic way: "I don't even have time to read the kind of short books you write," he said. "But a year ago I talked about you to my relatives in Careno." To amaze the doctor with my ignorance, I asked him where Careno was.

"It's in Italy, the north of Italy," he answered, scandalized. Then he lowered his eyes, as if in forgiveness. He asked me what my father's name was, my grandfather, my great-grandfather. I answered compliantly but soon got tired of so many questions and told him that there was no point in having this conversation—"My family is definitely descended from some bastard child." I told him: "We come from some *patrón* who didn't take responsibility." I told him that in my family we're all dark-skinned— the doctor himself was very white and fairly ugly, with that hygienic whiteness that in some people hardly seems real. Resigned to not finding any sign of encouragement from me, the doctor told me that every year he traveled to

Careno, where there are many people with our last name, since historically the family was quite inbred.

"There are lots of marriages between siblings and between cousins, so the genes aren't so good," he said.

"We don't have that problem," I told him. "In my branch of the family we treat our cousins with respect."

He laughed, or tried to laugh. I wanted, I'm not sure why, to apologize. But before I could say the sentence I was vaguely trying to formulate, the doctor asked about my symptoms. He was in a hurry now. He spent barely two minutes on my ailment, roundly denying I had the swine flu, as if reproaching me for even thinking it. He didn't even lecture me about how many cigarettes I smoke.

I went home a bit humiliated, with the same antiflu medicines as always, thinking about those families in far-off Careno, about what my face would be like white, washed-out, or about my distant desire, once upon a time, to study medicine. I imagined that same doctor, older than me in medical school, answering emphatically, annoyed: no, we're not related.

≫≫≫≪≪≪

Parents abandon their children. Children abandon their parents. Parents protect or forsake, but they always forsake. Children stay or go but they always go. And it's all unfair, especially the sound of the words, because the language is pleasing and confusing, because ultimately we would like to sing or at least whistle a tune, to walk alongside the stage whistling a tune. We want to be actors waiting patiently for the cue to walk onstage. But the audience left a long time ago.

>>»«««

Today I made up this joke:

"When I grow up I'm going to be a secondary character," a boy says to his father.

"Why?"

"Why what?"

"Why do you want to be a secondary character?"

"Because the novel is yours."

>>»«««

I'm writing in my parents' house. It's been a long time since I've been here. I prefer to see them in town, at lunchtime. But this time I wanted to watch the Chile-versus-Paraguay game with my father, thinking I could also refresh some details for the story while I was here. It's the trip in the novel, the frightened protagonist's trip home at the end of the long evening when he follows Raúl's supposed girlfriend. I wrote that passage thinking about a real trip I took more or less at that age.

One afternoon, after lunch, I was getting ready to go out when my father said no, I had to stay home and study English. I asked why, since I was getting good grades in English. "Because it isn't prudent for you to go out so much." He used that word, *prudent*, I remember exactly.

"And because I am your father and you have to obey me," he said.

It seemed brutal to me, but I studied, or at least I pretended to. At night, before going to sleep, still angry, I told my father that it made me so mad to be a kid and to have to ask permission for everything, that it would be better to be an orphan. I only said it to annoy him, but he gave me a sly look and went to talk to my mother. I could tell by her gestures as they approached that they didn't agree on the measure they were about to announce to me, but that I would have to abide by it anyway.

Before speaking to me they called my sister to witness the scene. My father addressed her first. He told her they had been living a lie. That until then they had believed she was the older sibling, but that they had just discovered she wasn't. "So, we're going to give your brother the keys to the house—you can go out and come home whatever time you want, from now on you're in charge of yourself," he told me, looking me in the eye. "No one will ask you where you're going or if you have homework or anything else."

So it was. I enjoyed those privileges for several weeks. They treated me like an adult, with only a few traces of irony. I grew desperate. I told my mother I was going very far away and she answered that I shouldn't forget to take my suitcase with me. I didn't take a suitcase, but one afternoon I anxiously boarded a random bus, prepared to stay on until the end of its route and with no plan for when I got there.

I didn't get to the end of the route, but I did almost reach the neighborhood where I live now. The trip took over an hour and when I got back they yelled at me a lot. That was what I wanted. I was happy to have my parents back. And I had also discovered a new world. A world I didn't like, but a new one.

That route doesn't exist anymore. Today I came by metro and then bus and I got to Maipú by way of Los Pajaritos. I'm always surprised at the number of Chinese restaurants on the avenue. For years now, Maipú has been a small big city, and the stores I frequented as a child are now bank branches or fast-food chains.

Before I got to my parents' house I took a detour to pass by Lucila Godoy Alcayaga. The street was closed off with an eye-catching electric gate, as was the passage Neftalí Reyes Basoalto. I didn't feel like asking anyone going by to let me in. I wanted to see Claudia's house, which in reality was, for a time, my friend Carla Andreu's house. I headed, then, for Aladdin. The neighborhood is full of attics now, second floors that look out of place, ostentatious roofs. No longer is it the dream of equality. Just the opposite. Lots of houses have been abused, and others are luxurious. Some of them look abandoned.

There were changes as well in my parents' house. I was struck most of all by the sight of a new bookshelf in the living room. I recognized the automotive encyclopedia, the BBC English course, and the old books put out by *Ercilla* magazine, with its collections of Chilean, Spanish, and world literatures. On the middle shelf there was also a series of novels by Isabel Allende, Hernán Rivera Letelier, Marcela Serrano, John Grisham, Barbara Wood, Carla Guelfenbein, and Pablo Simonetti, and closer to the floor were some books I read as a child for school: *The Löwensköld Ring* by Selma Lagerlöf, *Alsino* by Pedro Prado, *Michael Strogoff* by Jules Verne, *El ultimo grumete de la* Baquedano by Francisco Coloane, *Fermina Márquez* by Valéry Larbaud. Well. I wish I'd kept them myself, but I'm sure I forgot them in some box my parents found in the attic.

It was discomfiting to see those books there, hastily ordered on a red melamine shelf, flanked by posters of hunting scenes or sunrises and a faded reproduction of *Las Meninas* that has been in the house forever and that my father still proudly shows visitors: "This is the painter, Velásquez; the painter painted himself," he says.

"Thanks to that library, your mother has started reading and I have too, though of course I'd rather watch movies," said my father, and he turned on the TV right on time for the game. We celebrated goals by Mati Fernández and Humberto Suazo with a big pitcher of pisco sour and a couple bottles of wine. I drank much more than my father did. I've never seen him drunk, I thought, and for some reason I said it out loud to him.

"I *did* see my father drunk, many times," he answered abruptly, with a barely contained look of sadness.

"Stay over, your sister is coming to lunch tomorrow," my mother said. "You can't drive in the state you're in," she added, and I reminded her of something she always forgets: I don't have a car. "Oh," she said. "That's right. All the more reason you can't drive," she laughed. I like her laugh, especially when it comes suddenly, when it happens unexpectedly. It is serene and sweet at the same time.

I left home fifteen years ago, but I still feel a kind of strange pulse when I enter this room that used to be mine and is now a kind of storage room. At the back there's a shelf full of DVDs and photo albums jumbled in the corner next to my books, the books I've published. It strikes me as beautiful that they're here, next to the family mementos.

»»»«««

A little while ago, at two in the morning, I got up to make coffee and I was surprised to see my mother in the living room, drinking *mate* with a beginner's graceful movements.

"This is what I do now when I feel like smoking," she said with a smile. She smokes very little, five cigarettes a day, but since my father quit he doesn't let her smoke inside, and it's too cold to open the window.

"I'm going to smoke," I said. "Let's smoke. Dad can't stop you from smoking, you're too old for that now," I said.

"He only denies me cigarettes. I deny him lots of things—saturated fats, too much sugar. It's only fair."

Finally I convinced her and we shut ourselves up in a sort of small room they had built to house an immense new washing machine. She smoked with the same movement as always, so markedly feminine: the cigarette tilted downward, her hand palm out, very close to her mouth.

"What will I do," she said suddenly, "if tomorrow your father realizes we were smoking?"

"Tell him we didn't smoke. That if it smells it's because I smoke a lot. I smell like cigarettes. Tell him that. And then change the subject, tell him you're worried because you think I'm smoking too much, and I'm going to die of cancer."

"But that would be a lie," she said.

"It wouldn't be a lie," I answered, "because sooner or later I *am* going to die of cancer."

My mother let out a deep sigh and slowly shook her head. Then she said something astonishing: "No one in my life has ever made me laugh as much as you. You are the funniest person I've ever met. But you're also serious, and that was always disconcerting, it *is* disconcerting. You left home very young, and sometimes I wonder what life would be like if you hadn't left. There are kids your age who still live with their parents. I see them go by sometimes and I think of you."

"Life would have been worse," I said. "And those big babies are spoiled brats."

"Yes. It's true. And you're right. Life would be worse if you lived here. Before you left, your father and I used to fight a lot. But after you left, we didn't fight as much. Now we hardly ever fight."

I wasn't expecting that sudden moment of honesty. I

sat there thinking, disheartened, but right away she asked me, as if it were relevant: "Do you like Carla Guelfenbein?"

I didn't know how to answer. "I think she's pretty. I'd go out with her, but I wouldn't sleep with her," I said. "Maybe I'd kiss her, but I wouldn't sleep with her, or I'd sleep with her but I wouldn't kiss her." My mother pretended to be scandalized. The gesture looked beautiful on her.

"I'm asking if you like her writing."

"No, Mom. I don't like it."

"But I like her novel. *The Other Side of the Heart.*"

"*The Other Side of the Soul,*" I corrected her.

"That's it, *The Other Side of the Soul.* I identified with the characters, the book moved me."

"And how is it possible for you to identify with characters from another social class, with problems that aren't and could never be problems in your life, Mom?"

I spoke seriously, too seriously. I knew it wasn't appropriate to speak seriously, but I couldn't help it. She looked at me with a mixture of anger and compassion. With a little annoyance. "You're wrong," she said finally. "Maybe it's not my social class, I agree. But social classes have changed a lot, everyone says so, and when I read that novel I felt that yes, those were my problems. I know what I'm saying bothers you, but you should be a little more tolerant."

It seemed very strange that my mother would use that

word, *tolerant*. I went to sleep remembering my mother's voice saying: You should be a little more tolerant.

>>>«««

After lunch my sister insisted on driving me home. She got her license a year ago but she really learned to drive only last month. She didn't seem nervous, though. I was the nervous one. I chose to surrender, close my eyes and open them only when she shifted gears and the car stuttered too much. In moments of silence my sister accelerated, and when the conversation flowed she slowed down so much that other cars overtook us, horns sounding.

"I feel bad about what happened with your marriage," she told me, soon after we left the highway.

"That was a long time ago," I replied.

"But I hadn't told you that."

"We got back together recently." My sister's expression is something between incredulous and happy. I explain that for now it's all fragile, tentative, but that I feel good. That we want to do things better this time. That we're not living together again yet. She asks me why I didn't tell our parents. "That's exactly why," I say. "It's still too early to tell them."

Then she asks me if I'm going to write more books. I like the way she frames the question, since it implies the possibility that I could simply say no, enough already; and that's what I do think, sometimes, at the end of a bad night:

Soon I'll stop writing, just like that, and someday I'll have a distant memory of the time when I wrote books, the same way others remember the season they drove a taxi or worked selling dollars in Paseo Ahumada.

But I answer yes, and she asks me to tell her what the new book is about. I don't want to answer, and she realizes this and asks again. I tell her it's about Maipú, about the earthquake of '85, about childhood. She asks for more details, I give them to her. We reach my house and I invite her in; she doesn't want to come but she also doesn't want me to go. I know very well what she's going to ask.

"Am I in your book?" she finally says.

"No."

"Why not?"

I've thought about it. Of course I've thought about it. I've thought about it a lot. My answer is honest:

"To protect you," I say.

She looks at me skeptically, hurt. She looks at me with a little girl's expression.

"It's better not to be someone else's character," I say. "It's better not to be in any book."

"And are you in the book?"

"Yes. More or less. But it's my book. I couldn't not be in it. Even if I gave myself very different characteristics and a life very different from mine, I would still be in the book. I already made the decision not to protect myself."

"And are our parents in it?

"Yes. There are characters like our parents."

"And why not protect our parents, too?"

For that question, I don't have an answer. I suppose it's their lot, simply, to appear. To receive less than they gave, to attend a masked ball and not understand very well why they are there. I'm not capable of saying any of that to my sister.

"I don't know, it's fiction," I tell her. "I have to go, sis." I don't call her by her name. I call her "sis," give her a kiss on the cheek, and get out of the car.

Back home I spend a long time thinking of my sister, my big sister. I remember this poem by Enrique Lihn:

So the only child's the eldest of his brothers
and in his orphanhood has something
of what eldest means. As though
they too had died
those impossible younger brothers.

When we write we act like only children. As if we had been alone forever. Sometimes I hate this story, this profession that I can no longer leave. That now I'll never leave.

≫≫≫≪≪≪

I always thought I didn't have real childhood memories. That my history fit into a few lines. On one page, maybe. In large print. I don't think that anymore.

The family weekend has crushed my will. I find consolation in a letter that Yasunari Kawabata wrote to his friend Yukio Mishima in 1962: "Whatever your mother says, your writing is magnificent."

Just now I tried to write a poem, but I managed only these few lines:

Growing up, I meant to be a memory
But now I've had as much as I can bear
Of forever seeking out the beauty
In a tree that's been disfigured by the wind

The part I like is the beginning:

Growing up, I meant to be a memory.

LITERATURE OF THE
CHILDREN

I LEFT HOME AT THE END OF 1995, JUST AFTER
I turned twenty, but throughout my adolescence I yearned
to leave these overly clean sidewalks behind, to get away
from the boring streets where I grew up. I wanted a full and
dangerous life, or maybe I just wanted what some children
always want: a life without parents.

I lived in boardinghouses or small rooms and worked
wherever I could while I finished university. And when I
finished university I kept on working wherever I could, because I studied literature, which is what people do before
they end up working wherever they can.

Years later, however, already approaching thirty, I got
a job as a teacher and managed to establish myself to a
certain extent. I practiced a calm and dignified life: I spent
the afternoons reading novels or watching TV for hours,
smoking tobacco or marijuana, drinking beer or cheap
wine, listening to music or listening to nothing—because

sometimes I sat in silence for long stretches, as if waiting for something, for someone.

That's when I went back, when I returned. I wasn't expecting to find anyone, I wasn't looking for anything, but one summer night, a night like any other when I went out walking with long, sure steps, I saw the blue facade, the green gate, and the small square of dry grass just in front. Here it is, I thought. This is where I was. I said it out loud, incredulity in my voice. I remembered the scene exactly: the bus trip, the woman's neck, the store, the harrowing return trip, everything.

I thought of Claudia then, and also of Raúl and of Magali; I imagined or tried to imagine their lives, their destinies. But suddenly the memories shut off. For a second, without knowing why, I thought they must all be dead. For a second, not knowing why, I felt immensely alone.

In the following days I went back to the place almost obsessively. Intentionally or unconsciously, I directed my steps to the house and, sitting in the grass, I stared at the facade as night fell. First the streetlights would come on, and later, after ten, a small window on the second floor would light up. For days the only sign of life in that house was that faint light that appeared on the second floor.

One afternoon I saw a woman open the door and take out bags of garbage. Her face seemed familiar and at first I thought it was Claudia, although the image I still held of her was so remote that I could extrapolate many different faces from the memory. The woman had the cheekbones of a thin person, but she had gotten possibly irremediably fat. Her red hair formed a hard and shiny fabric, as if she had just dyed it. And in spite of that conspicuous appearance she seemed bothered by the simple fact that someone was looking at her. She walked as if her gaze were stuck to the sidewalk cracks.

I hoped to see her again. Some afternoons I brought a novel along, but I preferred books of poetry, since they allowed more breaks for spying. I was ashamed, but it also made me laugh to be a spy again. A spy who, once again, didn't know what he wanted to find.

ONE AFTERNOON I DECIDED TO RING THE BELL. When I saw the woman coming to answer I panicked, knowing I had no plan and I didn't even know how I should introduce myself. Stuttering, I told her I had lost my cat. She asked me his name, and I didn't know how to answer. She asked what the cat looked like. I said he was black, white, and brown.

"Then it's not a he, it's a she," said the woman.

"It's a he," I answered.

"If it's three colors it can't be a he. Tricolored cats are females," she said. And she added that in any case she hadn't seen any stray cats in the neighborhood recently.

The woman was going to close the door when I said, almost shouting: "Claudia."

"Who are you?" she asked.

I told her. I told her we had known each other in Maipú. That we had been friends.

She looked at me for a long time. I let myself be looked at. It's a strange sensation, when you're waiting for someone to recognize you. Finally she told me: "I know who you are. I'm not Claudia. I'm Ximena, Claudia's sister. And you're that boy who followed me that afternoon, Aladdin. That's what Claudia called you, we always laughed when we remembered you. Aladdin."

I didn't know what to say. I precariously understood that yes, Ximena was the woman I had followed so many years earlier. Raúl's supposed girlfriend. But Claudia had never told me she had a sister. I felt a weight, the need to find some opportune phrase. "I'd like to see Claudia," I said, in a small voice.

"I thought you were out looking for a cat. A girl cat."

"Yes," I answered. "But I've often thought, over the years, about that time in Maipú. And I'd like to see Claudia again."

There was hostility in Ximena's gaze. She was silent. I talked, nervously improvising, about the past, about the desire to recover the past.

"I don't know what you want to see Claudia for," said Ximena. "I don't think you'd ever understand a story like ours. Back then people were looking for missing persons, they looked for the bodies of people who had disappeared. I'm sure in those years you were looking for kittens or puppies, same as now."

I didn't understand her cruelty; it seemed excessive, unnecessary. All the same, Ximena took down my phone number. "When she gets here I'll give it to her," she said.

"And when do you think she's going to come?"

"Any minute now," she answered. "My father is about to die. When he dies, my sister will come from Yankee-land to cry over his corpse and ask for her part of the inheritance."

It struck me as ridiculous and juvenile to refer to the United States as Yankee-land, and at the same time I thought about that conversation with Claudia, in the Maipú Temple, about flags. Ultimately, fate took her to that country she disparaged as a child, I thought, and I also thought that I should leave, but I couldn't help but ask one last, polite question:

"How is Don Raúl?" I asked.

"I don't know how Don Raúl is. I'm sure he's fine. But my father is dying. Bye, Aladdin," she said. "You don't understand, you'll never understand anything, *huevón*."

I WALKED AROUND THE NEIGHBORHOOD SEVeral more times, but I looked at the house from far away; I didn't dare get closer. I often thought about that bitter

75

conversation with Ximena. Her words pursued me somehow. One night I dreamed I ran into her at the supermarket. I was working, promoting a new beer. She passed by with her cart full of cat food. She looked at me out of the corner of her eye. She recognized me but avoided saying hello.

I also thought about Claudia, but it was like thinking of a ghost, like thinking about someone who, in some way that is irrational yet nonetheless concrete, accompanies us. I didn't expect her to call. I couldn't imagine her sister giving her my number, telling her about that unexpected visit, Aladdin's strange apparition. But that's how it went: some months after that conversation with Ximena, early one morning, just before nine, Claudia called me. She was friendly. "It would be fun to see each other again," she said.

We met one November afternoon, at the Starbucks in La Reina. I'd like to remember each of her words now, with absolute precision, and write them down in this notebook with no additional commentary. I'd like to imitate her voice, to raise a camera to the gestures she made as she dived, fearlessly, into the past. I'd like someone else to write this book. For her to write it, perhaps. I'd like her to be at my house, right now, writing. But it's for me to write and here I am. And here I'll stay.

`YOU WEREN'T HARD TO RECOGNIZE," SAYS Claudia.

"You either," I answer, but for long minutes I'm distracted as I search for the face I have in my memory. I don't find it. If I'd seen her in the street I wouldn't have recognized her.

We go up to get our coffees. I don't usually go to Starbucks, and I'm surprised to see my name scrawled on the cup. I look at her cup, her name. She's not dead, I think suddenly, happily. She's not dead.

Claudia's hair is short now and her face is very thin. Her breasts are still meager and her voice sounds like a smoker's, though she smokes only when she's in Chile. "It seems like in the United States they don't let you smoke anywhere anymore," I say, suddenly content for the conversation to be simply social, routine.

"It's not that. It's weird. In Vermont I don't feel like smoking, but when I get to Chile I smoke like crazy," says Claudia. "It's like Chile is incomprehensible or intolerable unless I smoke."

"As if Chile were incendiary," I say, joking.

"Yes," says Claudia, without laughing. She laughs later. Ten seconds later she gets the joke.

At first the conversation follows the shy course of a

blind date, but sometimes Claudia speeds up and starts to talk in long sentences. The plot begins to clear up: "Raúl is my father," she says with no lead-up. "But his name was Roberto. The man who died three weeks ago, my father, was named Roberto."

I look at her astonished, but it isn't a pure astonishment. I receive the story as if expecting it. Because I do expect it, in some way. It's the story of my generation.

`I WAS BORN FIVE DAYS AFTER THE COUP, SEP-tember sixteenth, 1973," says Claudia in a kind of outpouring. The shadow of a tree falls capriciously over her mouth, so I don't see her lips moving. It's disturbing. I feel like a photograph is talking to me. I remember that beautiful poem "The eyes of this dead lady speak to me." But she moves her hands and life returns to her body. She isn't dead, I think again, and again I feel an immense happiness.

Magali and Roberto had Ximena when Roberto had just entered law school at the University of Chile. They lived separately until she got pregnant again and then, at the beginning of 1973, they got married and decided to live in La Reina while they looked for a place of their own. Magali was older. She had studied English at the Pedagogical Institute and she belonged to Allende's party, but she wasn't active. Roberto, on the other hand, was a committed activist, though he wasn't involved in any dangerous situations.

They spent the first years of the dictatorship terrified and ensconced in that house in La Reina. But toward the end of 1981 Roberto reconnected: he started circulating around certain places he had avoided up to then, and he quickly took on responsibilities, at first very minor ones, as an informant. Every morning he waited—on the steps of the National Library, on a bench in the Plaza de Armas, and even a few times at the zoo—for his contacts, and then he went back to work in a small office on Moneda Street.

Soon afterward Magali rented the house in Maipú and she went to live there with the girls. It was the best way to protect them, far away from everything, far from the world. Roberto, meanwhile, did take risks, but he changed his appearance constantly. At the beginning of 1984 he convinced his brother-in-law Raúl to leave the country and give him his identity. Raúl left Chile over the mountains and went to Mendoza, with no definite plan but with a bit of money to begin a new life.

It was then that Roberto took the house in Aladdin Street. Again, Maipú seemed like a safe place, where it was possible to not awaken suspicion. He lived very close to his wife and daughters and his new identity allowed him to see them more often, but caution came first. The girls almost never saw their father and Claudia didn't even know he lived close by. She only found out that night, the night of the earthquake.

LEARNING TO TELL HER STORY AS IF IT DIDN'T hurt. That was, for Claudia, growing up: learning to tell her story precisely, bluntly. But it's a trap to put it like that, as if the process ever ended. "Only now do I feel I can do it," says Claudia. "I tried for a long time. But now I've found a kind of legitimacy. A drive. Now I want someone, anyone, to ask me out of nowhere: Who are you?"

I'm the one asking, I think. I'm the stranger who's asking. I was expecting a meeting heavy with silences, a series of disconnected phrases that later on, like when I was a child, I would have to put together and decipher. But no, on the contrary: Claudia wants to talk. "When I was on the plane coming here," she says, "I looked at the clouds for a long time. It seemed like they were drawing something faint and disconcerting but at the same time recognizable. I thought about a kid scribbling on paper or the drawings my mother made when she was on the phone. I don't know if it happened once or many times, but I have this image of my mother scribbling on paper while she talked on the phone.

"Then I looked," says Claudia, "at the flight attendants

smoothing their skirts while they talked and laughed at the back of the aisle, and at the stranger dozing next to me with a self-help book open on his chest. And then I thought how my mother had died ten years ago, how my father had just died, and instead of silently honoring their deaths I felt an imperative need to talk. The wish to say: I. The vague, strange pleasure, even, of answering: 'My name is Claudia and I'm thirty-three years old.'"

The thing she most wished for during that long trip to Santiago was for the stranger traveling next to her to wake up and ask: Who are you, what's your name? She wanted to answer him quickly, cheerfully, even flirtatiously. She wanted to tell him, like they do in novels: My name is Claudia, I'm thirty-three years old, and this is my story. And then begin to tell it, finally, as if it didn't hurt.

By now it is night, and we are still sitting on the cafe terrace. "You're tired of listening to me," she says suddenly. I deny it with a sharp shake of the head. "But later I'm going to listen to you," she says. "And I promise that when I get tired of listening to you, you won't realize it. I'll pretend really well," she says, smiling.

CLAUDIA ARRIVED WHEN THE WAKE WAS JUST about to start. She accepted people's condolences with something like boredom: she preferred silent hugs, without those terrible phrases ready-made for the occasion. After the funeral she unpacked her suitcases in what had once been her room. She thought how she was, after all, coming home; how the only space she had ever really felt comfortable in was that small room in the house in La Reina, although that stability hadn't lasted long, barely a few years toward the end of the eighties when her grandmother, her mother, and her father were all still alive.

As if she had cruelly guessed Claudia's thoughts, as if she'd spent a long time waiting to pronounce certain sentences, Ximena came in suddenly and said: "This isn't your house anymore. You can stay here a few weeks, but don't get used to it. I took care of Dad, so the house is mine; I'm not going to sell it, don't even think about it. And it would be a lot better if you found a hotel."

Claudia agreed, thinking that as the days passed her sister would regain her calm, her senses. She lay on the bed to read a novel; she wanted to forget that bitter conversation and be carried along by the plot, but it was impossible, because the book was about parents who abandoned their children or children who abandoned their parents. Ultimately, that's what all books are about, she thought.

She went to the living room, where Ximena was watching TV, and sat down next to her. Gregory House was in the middle of saying something crude to Dr. Cuddy, and Claudia remembers that she and Ximena laughed in unison. Then she made tea and offered Ximena a cup. She thought her sister had the face of someone who had suffered not just a day or a week but all her life. "I'm sorry," said Ximena as she took the tea. "You can stay here as long as you like, but don't ask me to sell the house. It's all I have, all *we* have."

Claudia was about to reply with some opportune, empty phrase: we have each other, we'll get through this together, something along those lines. But she held back. It wouldn't have been true. It had been a long time since they'd been able to live together without animosity. "Let's talk about the house later," she said.

WE WALK WITHOUT A DESTINATION BUT I don't realize it, I simply accompany Claudia, thinking we're going somewhere. It's very late now, the movie theater is closed; we stop to look at the movie posters as if we were a couple out looking for something to do.

"It's good to live close to a cinema," she says, and we start talking animatedly about movies. We discover coincidences that inevitably bring us back to real life, to our youth, to childhood. Because we can't, we don't know how to talk about a movie or a book anymore; the moment has come when movies and novels don't matter, only the time when we saw them, read them: where we were, what we were doing, who we were then.

While we walk silently I think about those names:

83

Roberto, Magali, Ximena, Claudia. I ask about her grandmother's name. "Mercedes," Claudia answers. I think they are serious names. Even Claudia suddenly seems like a serious name. Beautiful, simple, and serious. I ask her what year her grandmother died. "In 1995, a year before my mother," says Claudia. And she talks about another death as well, of someone important, someone she never met: her father's cousin Nacho, the doctor. Nacho was arrested and he never came back. Roberto and Magali always talked about him as if he were alive, but he was dead.

They told her when she was little, and later—for many years—they continued telling her the story of the fever, which wasn't even a story. It was merely a moment, the last one, although no one knew it would be the last one: in 1974, when Claudia had been alive for eleven months, Nacho went to see her because she had been sick for too many hours. The fever broke immediately. "It's a miracle," said the adults that afternoon, laughing. And that's what it became, a slight, insignificant miracle: to lower a little girl's fever, only that, on the afternoon when they saw him for the last time—for they never saw him dead, his body never appeared.

"In my family there are no dead," I say. "No one has died. Not my grandparents, not my parents, not my cousins, no one."

"You never go to the cemetery?"

"No, I never go to the cemetery," I answer with a complete sentence, as if I were learning to speak a foreign language and I'd been instructed to answer that way.

"I have to go, I'd rather get back early to my father's house." A gesture of her lips gives her away immediately: it's not her father's house anymore, now it's hers and Ximena's. I go with her, hoping she'll invite me in for coffee, but she says goodbye at the gate with a bright smile and a hug.

On the way back home I remember a scene in college, one afternoon when we were smoking weed and drinking a sticky wine with melon. I'd spent the afternoon with a group of classmates, and we were exchanging family stories in which death appeared with urgent insistence. Of all those present I was the only one who came from a family with no dead, and that realization filled me with a strange bitterness: my friends had grown up reading the books that their dead parents or siblings left behind in the house. But in my family there were no dead and there were no books.

I come from a family with no dead, I thought as my classmates told their childhood stories. At that moment I had a strong memory of Claudia, but I didn't want or didn't dare to tell her story. It wasn't mine. I knew little, but at least I knew that: no one could speak for someone else. That although we might want to tell other people's stories, we always end up telling our own.

I WANT TO LET A FEW DAYS GO BY BEFORE I call her and suggest getting together again. But I'm impatient and I do it right away. She doesn't seem surprised. We arrange to meet the next morning, in Intercommunal Park. I get there early but I see her from far away, sitting on a bench and reading. She looks beautiful. She is wearing a jean skirt and an old black shirt with big blue letters that say LOVE SUCKS.

Some kids playing hooky come over to ask for a light. "I didn't smoke at that age," Claudia says to me.

"I did," I answer. I tell her that I started smoking at twelve. Sometimes when I was walking with my father and he lit a cigarette, I would ask him to put it out, saying it was bad for him and he was going to die of cancer. I did it to trick him, so he wouldn't suspect that I smoked too, and he would look at me apologetically and explain that smoking was a vice and that vices were the signs of human weakness. I remember how I liked it when he suddenly confessed his weakness, his vulnerability.

"I, on the other hand, only saw my father smoke one time," says Claudia as we wander through the park. "One day I got home early from school and he was in the living room talking to my mother. I was so happy to see him. I lived hoping to see him. My father hugged me and maybe it was a long hug, but I felt like he let go of me quickly, as if we weren't allowed to have that contact, either. Then I realized he had a lit cigarette in his right hand. It unsettled me. It was like he really was a different person. As if Roberto wasn't smoking, Raúl was."

"He also smoked the night of the earthquake, with my dad," I remind her. "I think my dad offered yours a cigarette and they smoked together, and talked."

"Really?" asks Claudia, incredulous, as she fixes her hair. "I don't remember that. But I remember you," she says.

"Were you really looking for someone to spy on your father?"

"No," she says. "I didn't know my father lived there. It was a very ambiguous situation. The night of the earthquake I was alone with my mother, because Ximena had gone to my grandmother's. Back then Ximena spent a lot of time with Grandma, she practically lived with her. A brick wall fell and broke the big front window, so we couldn't sleep there. I remember we were desperate, we went out walking and I didn't know we were looking for my dad, and that he was also looking for us. I don't know if we took different routes or if we passed each other by. When we finally saw him on a corner I couldn't believe it. I had a little flashlight, a toy, which they'd given to me years before. I remember I shined it on his face and saw his eyes were a little wet. We hugged and then he brought us to the fire. Before dawn the three of us left for the house in La Reina, in his car."

"The Fiat 500," I say.

"The Fiat 500, yes," she answers.

It affected Claudia a lot to find out that her father lived close by. She was sick of secrets, and at the same time she intuited numerous dangers, huge and imprecise dangers. She liked seeing me there, with the adults around the fire. "You stayed quiet, you observed. I was like that too, silent. I started following you without a clear purpose, and little by little I came up with a plan."

Neither did Claudia know exactly why she was spying, what she wanted to find out. But when she learned, through me, that Roberto was hiding people in the house, she wasn't surprised.

"And did you think your father had a lover?"

"I didn't know what to think. When we talked that time I lost it, the truth is I knew very little about my father. Then I thought it had to be Ximena. I didn't figure you would follow her like that, but it made me so mad to know she saw my father more than I did. She and my father, we said later, half joking, were the revolutionaries. My mother and I, on the other hand, were the reactionaries. We could joke about it, but it still hurt and I guess it even hurts now."

When Ximena saw that a boy, that I, was following her, she had no doubt that her sister had sent me. Claudia found herself obliged to confess that she was the one who had asked me to spy on her father. They scolded her, emphatically at first and then lovingly. An argument began in which everyone blamed someone else. "I didn't want to be responsible for those shouting matches, but I was," says Claudia, and then there is a long and uncertain pause. For ten minutes it seems like she is about to speak, but she can't bring herself to. Finally, she says: "I really feel like eating some chocolate ice cream."

WE HAVEN'T SEEN EACH OTHER FOR A WEEK but I call her every day, and I have the impression Claudia waits for those calls. One night, very late, she's the one who calls me. "I'm outside," she says. "Ximena threw me out. She says the house is hers. She called me a foreigner and a whore."

Claudia cries with the precise movements of someone trying not to sob. I hug her, I offer her tea, and we listen to music while I think about the reasons Ximena might have for calling her a whore. I almost ask, but I keep quiet. I tell her she can stay with me, that there's only one bed but I can sleep on the armchair. "It'll just be one night," she answers. "But I want us to sleep together. That way my sister will be right, I'll be a whore."

Claudia's eyes brighten: she gets her laughter back, her beauty. I offer her some cheese and I open a bottle of wine. We talk and drink for hours. I like how she moves around the house. She occupies the space as if recognizing it. She changes one chair for another, she stands up, suddenly she sits on the floor and stays for a while with her hands on her ankles.

I tell her it seems incredible that Ximena threw her out.

"She didn't throw me out, really," she answers. "We had a bad argument, but I could have stayed at the house. I wanted to leave, it's really hard for me to live with her."

I ask her if Ximena was always like that. She tells me no, that their father's illness changed her. That in his last years she gave up everything to take care of him. "Now that my father is gone she doesn't know what to do, she doesn't know how to live. But I guess it's more complicated than that," says Claudia, and she stares fixedly at the lamp in the living room, as if following the movement of a moth.

I ask her why she went to the United States. "I don't know," she answers. "I wanted to go, I wanted to leave. My father wanted me to go too, he was already sick by then, but he wanted me to go," says Claudia, taking on a confessional tone again. "He supported me, above all, during Ximena's attacks. But Ximena wanted me to go, too. In some way she fantasized about that ending: her taking care of my father to the end and me rushing back, full of guilt, for his funeral.

"I don't know when, years ago," Claudia adds, "Ximena constructed the story that I was the evil sister who wanted to take everything from her. And maybe it's too late to make peace now. Because Ximena is right, in a way. She stayed because she wanted to stay. But she stayed," says Claudia. "In some way my father had to choose which of his daughters' lives to fuck over. And he chose her. And I was saved."

I ask her if she is really full of guilt.

"I don't feel guilty," she answers. "But I feel that lack of guilt as if it were guilt."

"Are you going to go back to the States?"

Two weeks earlier, the afternoon of our reencounter, Claudia told me she had completed a master's in environmental law in Vermont, and she would rather look for work there, and that she had been living with an Argentine boyfriend for a long time. But now she pauses before answering.

"Sometimes I doubt it," she says finally. "Sometimes I think I should come back to Chile for good," she says. It seems to me that she doesn't know why she says it. I don't believe her. I don't think Claudia is seriously considering the possibility of staying. I think Claudia is simply looking for something, and as soon as she finds it she will go back to the United States.

She looks tired and relieved at the same time. And she is a bit drunk. As we have sex she smiles, showing her teeth a little bit. It's a beautiful and strange gesture. I think I will remember it. That I will miss it.

We sleep little, only two or three hours. Then the noise of cars, of voices, starts up. People leave for work, for school. We make orange juice, and while we eat breakfast she looks at her e-mail on my computer. She finds a message from Ximena. *I'm not going to sell the house, don't incist*, it says, and Claudia can't believe it: "It says incist, with *c*, really." For a millisecond she thinks it's terrible that Ximena would make that kind of mistake and right away she is ashamed, because it's even worse that, under the circumstances, she would care about something so stupid as a spelling mistake.

The house is not for sale, Ximena continues. *It's my house now. Now more than ever*, she says.

I'm not going to insist, thinks Claudia: it doesn't make sense. Deep down she understands why Ximena is attached to the house, though she thinks it would be better to sell it and split the money. She thinks that being so close to the past isn't good for anyone. That the past never stops hurting, but we can help it by finding a different place.

"But maybe it's too soon to talk about pain," she says to me while I look at the traces of wine on her lips. Suddenly she seems very young to me: twenty-five, twenty-six, definitely no more than thirty.

I GO TO THE UNIVERSITY, TEACH A NOT-SO-good class, go home. I had imagined the scene, but it still surprises me to open the door and see Claudia stretched out in the easy chair. "Your beauty does me good," I say to her, without thinking about it much. She looks at me cautiously and then lets out a guffaw, but she comes over, puts her arms around me, and we end up screwing standing up in a corner of the kitchen.

Afterward, we make noodles and put together a sauce with a little cream and some scallions. The sauce turns out a bit dry and the truth is neither one of us is hungry.

"Sometimes, when I look at the food on my plate," says Claudia, "I remember that expression, the answer my mother and grandmother would always give me: Shut up and eat." They'd made something new, some unfamiliar stew that didn't look good, and Claudia wanted to know what it was. Her mother and grandmother would answer in unison: Shut up and eat.

It was a joke, of course, a wise one, even. But that's how Claudia felt as a child: that strange things were happening and they were living with the pain, they struggled with a long and imprecise sadness, and nonetheless it was better not to ask questions. To ask was risking that they would answer the same way: Shut up and eat.

Later the time for questions came. The decade of the nineties was the time of questions, in her opinion, and right away she says, "I'm sorry, I don't want to sound like those quack sociologists you see on TV, but that's how those years were: I sat down and talked to my parents for hours, asked them for details, I made them remember, and I repeated those memories as if they were my own." In some terrible, secret way she was seeking her place in their story.

"We didn't ask in order to know," Claudia says to me as we collect the plates and clear the table: "We asked in order to fill an emptiness."

`SOMETIMES XIMENA REMINDS ME OF MY mother," says Claudia over cups of tea. "It's not a physical resemblance, really. It's her voice, the tone of her voice," she says.

She thinks about those moments when her mother had no other recourse but to talk. She called the girls to her, she took her time over her words, as if tuning in little by little to a sweet, calm tone—a careful tone, artificial. Then, as if conducting a ceremony, she spoke clearly. She modulated. She met their eyes.

One afternoon in 1984 she spoke to them separately. First she called Ximena into the kitchen and closed the door. It was strange for the conversation to take place in the kitchen. She had asked her mother about it shortly before her death. "Why did you want to talk to us in the kitchen that afternoon?"

"I don't know," said her mother. "Maybe because I was nervous."

The conversation with Ximena didn't last long. She quickly reemerged and ran outside, and Claudia couldn't see her face. In light of the circumstances, the five-year difference between the sisters became an insurmountable distance. Ximena was argumentative and irascible, but in the end she was always on the adults' side, while Claudia only understood things halfway.

"Then it was my turn," says Claudia, and she pauses in a way that seems dramatic. I think she's about to break down, but no, she just needed that pause. "I don't remember her words very well," she continues. "I guess she told me the truth, or something like the truth. I understood that there were good people and bad people, and we were good people. That good people were sometimes persecuted for thinking differently. For their ideas. I don't even know if I knew what an idea was back then, but in some way, that afternoon I found out."

Her mother talked to her in a soft, generous intonation: For a while you can't call your father Dad. He's going to cut his hair like your uncle Raúl's, he's going to shave his beard so he'll look a little more like your uncle Raúl. Claudia didn't understand, but she knew she had to understand. She knew that everyone else, including her sister, understood more than she did. And it hurt her to have to accept that. She asked her mother how long she would have to stop calling her father Dad. "I don't know. Maybe a short time. Maybe a long time. But I promise you that you're going to be able to call him Dad again."

"Do you swear?" said Claudia unexpectedly.

"Catholic families swear, in our family we only promise," said her mother. "But I promise you."

"I want you to swear it," the girl said.

"All right, I swear to you," her mother conceded, and she added that Claudia would always know that the man she called uncle was her father. That was enough. That was the important thing.

AT THE BEGINNING OF 1998, CLAUDIA'S FATHER got his identity back. It was the party's decision. With the referendum coming up, they needed activists who were publicly committed to practical tasks. Magali went to the airport with her two daughters. The situation was absurd. A week earlier Roberto had left for Buenos Aires with Raúl's identity and now he was returning as Roberto. He had cut his hair and sideburns a little and he was soberly dressed in blue jeans and a white shirt. He smiled a lot and at one point Claudia thought he seemed like a new man.

They didn't have to pretend so elaborately, but her

96

mother insisted: the same way she used to look at Claudia reproachfully when she called her father Dad, now she urged her, to an almost ridiculous extent, to say "Dad." On the plane there were people who actually had been in exile. Claudia remembers having felt a certain bitterness at seeing the families hug, crying in those long, legitimate embraces. For a moment she thought, and was immediately ashamed for thinking it, that the others were also faking. That what they were regaining was not the people but their names. They were undoing, at last, the distance between bodies and names. But no. There were real emotions around her. And when they got home, she felt that her emotion was real as well.

"It's a terrible story," I tell her, and she looks at me, surprised.

"No," she answers, and she says my name several times, as if I had been asleep for a long time and she wanted to wake me up little by little. "My story isn't terrible. That's what Ximena doesn't understand: our story isn't terrible. There was pain, and we'll never forget that pain, but we also can't forget the pain of others. Because we were protected, in the end; because there were others who suffered more, who suffer more."

We walk along Grecia Avenue past the College of Philosophy, and then I remember a story or hundreds of stories from that time, but I feel a little stupid, it seems like anything I could talk about would be trivial. We reach the National Stadium. The largest detention center in 1973 was always, for me, no more than a soccer field. My first memories of it are happy, sportive ones. I'm sure that I ate my first ice cream in the stadium's stands.

Claudia's first memory of the stadium is also happy. In 1977 it was announced that Chespirito, the Mexican comedian, would bring the entire cast of his show to perform at the National Stadium. Claudia was four years old then; she watched Chespirito's show and she liked it a lot.

Her parents refused to take her at first, but finally they gave in. The four of them went, and Claudia and Ximena had a great time. Many years later Claudia found out that for her parents that day had been torture. They had spent every moment thinking how absurd it was to see the stadium filled with laughing people. Throughout the entire show they had thought only, obsessively, about the dead.

EVERY ONCE IN A WHILE CLAUDIA SUGGESTS that she look for a hotel or go to a friend's house, but I insist on keeping her here. I can't offer much, but I want this time to continue at any cost. Some days aren't as good, but an agreeable routine starts to emerge. In the morning I go to the university while Claudia goes out walking or stays home thinking, mostly about the future. In the afternoon we have sex or watch movies, and night catches us by surprise, talking and laughing.

Sometimes I think she wants to stay, that she wants life to consist only of this, no more. It's what I want. I want to make her desire a life here. I want to entangle her again in the world from which she fled. I want to make her believe that she fled, that she forced her story in order to lose herself in the conventions of a comfortable and supposedly happy life. I want to make her hate that placid future in Vermont. In short, I behave like an asshole.

It's better to understand that time like one understands a brief summary in the TV guide: after twenty years, two childhood friends randomly reencounter each other and fall in love. But we aren't friends. And there is no love, not really. We sleep together. We screw wonderfully well and I'll never forget her dark, warm, firm body. But it isn't love that unites us. Or it is love, but love of memory.

We are united by a desire to regain the scenes of secondary characters. Unnecessary scenes that were reasonably discarded, and which nonetheless we collect obsessively.

CLAUDIA INSISTS THAT WE GO TO MAIPÚ. SHE says she wants to meet my parents. She wants to walk down those streets again. I don't think it's a good idea, but in the end I agree.

In the plaza she recognizes some monuments, some trees, the long stairs leading to the public pool, but not much more. Where the supermarket used to be, there is now something that looks like a municipal building.

We head now for the neighborhood where she used to live. They've closed off the passages with an eye-catching electric gate. Lucila Godoy Alcayaga and Neftalí Reyes Basoalto look like more exclusive streets now, at least exclusive enough to share in the paranoia about crime. There are many cars parked inside.

We manage to slip in behind some children on bicycles. Claudia looks at the house in silence for a moment, but then she rings the bell. "We're looking for a cat," she tells a man who comes out with his shirt untucked, as if he had been undressing. Claudia explains that it's a white cat with black spots. The man looks at her curiously; I'm sure he finds her desirable.

"I haven't seen a black-and-white cat, I see in color," he says, and I think how it's been many years since I heard such a lame joke. We laugh anyway, nervously.

The house is now a strange apricot color and instead of Persian blinds there are horrible flowered curtains. But it was never a pretty house; "It wasn't even a real house," says Claudia, with a calm sadness.

We decide to go, but we can't get out—the electric gate is locked. We buzz again but the man doesn't answer. We stay there for a while, like melancholy prisoners caressing the bars. In the meantime I call my parents. They're waiting for me. For us.

I'M SURPRISED TO SEE A BOOKSHELF IN THE LIV-
ing room. It's overflowing. "Thanks to that library your
mother has started to read and I have too, although you
know I'd rather watch movies," says my father. He doesn't
look at Claudia, but he is extremely polite, cautious.

The afternoon passes in a slow conversation that, at
certain moments, takes on shape to the rhythm of the pisco
sours we are drinking. We plan to leave, but my mother
starts to make dinner with slices of meat, duchess pota-
toes, and a vegetarian alternative.

"I'm not vegetarian," says Claudia when my mother
asks her.

"How odd, my son has always liked vegetarians," says
my mother. I start to get mad, but I let it pass when Claudia laughs naturally, warmly.

In spite of that joke, my parents avoid asking about the
details of our relationship. I told them on the phone only
that I would be bringing someone. I guess it seemed interesting or pleasant that I would want to introduce a girlfriend to them. It annoys me that the situation could be
seen that way: the son introducing a girlfriend. It isn't that,
we didn't come for that. I don't know what we did come
for, but we didn't come for that.

We talk about a recent series of robberies in the neighborhood. It's rumored that the thief lives around here. That it's one of the kids who grew up in our neighborhood. One who didn't succeed. One who was always something of a thief. "I've never stolen anything," says my father, suddenly. "Not even when I was little. We were very poor, I sold vegetables at a stall in the market." He looks at Claudia, conscious that he has told the story of his childhood a thousand times. He says that not even at the height of desperation would he steal. That back then he had friends who stole: "They were my friends, I loved them, but I hope they've ended up in jail," he says. "Otherwise society wouldn't function."

At what moment, I think, did my father change so much? Upon thinking this I immediately question it: I don't know if he has actually changed or if he was always like this. "I've stolen, I've stolen a lot," I say, to annoy him. At first my father laughs.

"Sure, you took money from my wallet, but that's not stealing."

"That *is* stealing," I answer seriously, sententiously. "Stealing from your father is still stealing. And I've also stolen books. One week I stole eighteen books." I say eighteen so it will sound excessive but still true, but really it was three and I felt so guilty I never went back to that bookstore. But I stand behind what I said, I don't take it back, and my father looks at me severely. He looks at me the way a father would look at a thieving son—a son already lost to him, in jail, on visitors' day.

My mother tries to ease the tension. "Who hasn't stolen at some time in their life?" she says, and slips into some anecdote from her childhood, looking at Claudia. She asks if she has ever stolen anything. Claudia answers that she hasn't, but if she was desperate maybe she would.

Claudia says that her head hurts. I ask her to go lie down. We go to the room that was mine as a child. I make up the sofa bed and hug Claudia; she lies back and closes her eyes, her eyelids trembling slightly. I kiss her, I promise her that as soon as she feels better we will leave. "I don't want to leave," she says unexpectedly. "I want to stay here, I think we need to sleep here tonight, don't ask me why," she says. I discover then that she isn't sick. I feel confused.

I go over to the little shelf holding the old family photo albums. That's what these albums are for, I think: to make us believe we were happy as children. To show ourselves that we don't want to accept how happy we were. I turn the pages slowly. I show Claudia a very old picture of my father getting off a plane, with long hair and very thick lenses blurring his eyes.

"Go back to the table," Claudia says, or requests. "I want to be alone for a few hours." She doesn't say for a while or for a bit. She says she wants to be alone for a few hours.

MY MOTHER REHEATS THE FOOD IN THE MI-
crowave while my father tunes the radio in search of a
classical music station—he's never liked it but he thinks it's
the appropriate music for dinner. He stands there, turning
the dial; he is upset and he doesn't want to look at me. "Sit
down, Dad, we're talking," I say with sudden authority.

While we eat I ask my parents if they remember the
night of the 1985 earthquake, if they remember our neighbor Raúl. My mother gets the neighbors and their families
confused, while my father remembers Raúl perfectly. "I
understand he was a Christian Democrat," he says, "although it was also rumored he was something more than
that."

"How so?"

"I don't know, it seems he was a Socialist, or a Communist, even."

"Communist like my grandfather?"

"My father wasn't a Communist. My father was a
worker, that's all. Raúl must have been something more
dangerous. But no, I don't know. He seemed peaceful
enough. Anyway, if Piñera wins the elections, the party's
over for Raúl. I'm sure he's lived high on the hog off those
corrupt and chaotic governments."

He says it to provoke me. I let him talk. I let him say a

few simplistic and bitter phrases. "They've had their hands in our pockets all these years," he says. "Those Concertación people are a bunch of thieves," he says. "A little order will do this country good." And then comes the feared pronouncement I'd been waiting for, the line that I can't, that I will not, allow to be crossed: "Pinochet was a dictator and all, he killed some people, but at least back then there was order."

I look him in the eyes. At what moment, I think, at what moment did my father turn into this? Or was he always like this? Was he always like this? I think it forcefully, with a severe and painful theatricality: Was he always this way?

My mother doesn't agree with what my father has said. Really, she more or less agrees, but she wants to do something to keep from spoiling the evening. "The world is much better now," she says. "Things are good. And Michelle is doing the best she can."

I can't help asking my father if in those years he was a Pinochet supporter. I've asked him that question hundreds of times, since I was a teenager; it's almost a rhetorical question, but he's never admitted it—why not admit it? I think. Why deny it for so many years, why deny it still?

My father sits in sullen, deep silence. Finally he says that no, he wasn't a Pinochet supporter, that he learned as a child that no one was going to save us.

"Save us from what?"

"Save us. Give us food to eat."

"But you *had* food to eat. We had food to eat."

"It's not about that," he says.

The conversation becomes unbearable. I get up to go check on Claudia. I stare at her intensely, but she goes on turning pages as if she doesn't notice I'm there. By now she's gone through half the albums. Her gaze absorbs, devours the images. Sometimes she smiles, sometimes her face becomes so serious that a sadness descends on me. No, I don't feel sadness: I feel fear.

I go back to the table; the vanilla ice cream is melting on my plate. I tell them in a low but very fast voice, so fast that the details become unintelligible, that Claudia was Raúl's daughter but for years she had to pretend she was his niece. That Raúl was really named Roberto. I don't know what I am hoping for by telling them. But I'm hoping for something, looking for something.

"It's a complicated story, but a good one," says my father, after a not very long silence.

"Are you fucking with me? A good story? It's a painful story."

"It's a painful story, but it's over now. Claudia is alive. Her parents are alive."

"Her parents are dead," I say.

"Were they killed by the dictatorship?"

"No."

"And how did they die?"

"Her mother died of a cerebral hemorrhage and her father of cancer."

"Poor Claudia," says my mother.

"But they didn't die for political reasons," says my father.

"But they're dead."

"But you're alive," he says. "And I bet you'll use such a good story in a book."

"I'm not going to write a story about them. I'm going to write about you two," I say, with a strange smile on my face. I can't believe what has just happened. I hate being the son who recriminates his parents, over and over again. But I can't help it.

I look straight at my father and he turns his face away. Then I see in his profile the shine of a contact lens and his slightly irritated right eye. I remember the scene, repeated countless times during my childhood: my father kneeling down, desperately searching for a contact lens that has just fallen out. We would all help him look, but he wanted to find it for himself and it was an enormous effort.

JUST AS CLAUDIA WANTED, WE STAY AT MY parents' house. At two in the morning I get up to make coffee. My mother is in the living room, drinking *mate*.

She offers me some, I accept. I think how I've never drunk *mate* with her before. I don't like the taste of sweetener but I suck hard on the straw; I burn myself a little.

"I was afraid of him," my mother says.

"Who?"

"Ricardo. Rodolfo."

"Roberto."

"That's it, Roberto. I could tell he was mixed up in politics."

"Everyone was mixed up in politics, Mom. You, too. Both of you. By not participating you supported the dictatorship." I feel that there are echoes in my language, there are hollows. I feel like I'm speaking according to a behavior manual.

"But we were never, your father and I, either for or against Allende, or for or against Pinochet."

"Why were you afraid of Roberto?"

"Well, I don't know if it was fear. But now you're telling me he was a terrorist."

"He wasn't a terrorist. He hid people, he helped people who were in danger. And he also helped pass information."

"And that doesn't seem like much to you?"

"It seems like the least he could do."

"But those people he hid were terrorists. They planted bombs. They planned attacks. That's reason enough to be afraid."

"Fine, Mom, but dictatorships don't fall just like that. The struggle was necessary."

"What do you know about those things? You hadn't even been born yet when Allende was in power. You were just a baby during those years."

I've heard that comment many times. You hadn't even been born. This time, though, it doesn't hurt. In a way, it makes me laugh. Just then my mother asks me, as if it were relevant:

"Do you like Carla Guelfenbein?"

I don't know how to answer. I say no. "I don't like those books, those kinds of books," I say.

"Well, we don't like the same kinds of books. I liked her novel *The Other Side of the Soul*. I identified with the characters, it moved me."

"And how is that possible, Mom? How can you identify with characters from another social class, with conflicts that aren't, that could never be, conflicts in your life?"

I speak in earnest, very seriously. I feel like I shouldn't speak so seriously. That it isn't appropriate. That I'm not going to solve anything by making my parents face up to the past. That I'm not going to achieve anything by taking away my mother's right to freely give her opinion on a book. She looks at me with a mixture of anger and compassion. With a little exasperation.

"You're wrong," she says. "Maybe it isn't my social class, fine, but social classes have changed a lot, everyone says so. And reading that novel I felt that yes, those *were* my problems. I understand that what I'm saying bothers you, but you should be a little more tolerant."

"I just said I didn't like that novel. And that it was strange that you would feel you identified with characters from another social class."

"And Claudia?"

"What about Claudia?"

"Is Claudia from your social class? What social class are you from, now? She lived in Maipú, but she wasn't from here. She looks more refined. You also look more refined than us. No one would say you were my son."

"I'm sorry," says my mother before I can answer the question, which, in any case, I wouldn't know how to answer. She gives me more *mate* and lights two cigarettes with the same match. "We're going to smoke inside here, even though your father doesn't like it." She passes one to me.

"It isn't your fault," she says. "You left home very young, at twenty-two."

"At twenty, Mom."

"At twenty, twenty-two, it doesn't matter. Very young. I sometimes think about what life would be like if you had stayed home. Some kids do. That thief boy, for example. He stayed here and became a thief. Others stayed too, and now they're engineers. That's life: you become a thief or an engineer. But I don't really know what you became."

"I don't know what my father became," I say, practically involuntarily.

"Your father has always been a man who loves his family. That's what he was, that's what he is."

"And what would life have been like if I had stayed, Mom?"

"I don't know."

"It would have been worse," I answer.

My mother nods. "Maybe it's better for us to be farther apart," she says. "I like how you are. I like that you defend your ideas. And I like that girl, Claudia, for you, even if she isn't from your social class."

She carefully puts out her cigarette and washes the ashtray before going to bed. I open the door and sit on the threshold. I want to look at the night, look for the moon, and to finish off in long gulps the whiskey I've just poured myself. I lean on my parents' car, a new Hyundai truck. The alarm goes off and my father gets up. I'm moved by the sight of him in his pajamas. He asks me if I'm drunk. "A little," I answer in a faint voice. "Just a little."

It's very late, five in the morning. I go up to the room. Claudia is sleeping, I lie down next to her; I move, wanting to wake her up. It's not just a little: I'm drunk. The darkness is almost complete and yet I can feel her gaze on my forehead and my chest. She strokes my neck, I bite her shoulder. "We can't miss this chance," she says, "to make love in your parents' house." Her body moves in the darkness as the day breaks.

AT EIGHT IN THE MORNING WE DECIDE TO leave. I go to my parents' room to say goodbye. I see them sleeping in an embrace. It's a weighty image for me. I feel ashamed, happy, and discomfited. I think that they are the beautiful survivors of a lost world, of an impossible world. My father wakes up and asks me to wait. He wants to give me some shirts he's getting rid of. There are six, they don't look old; I can tell they'll be too small for me but I accept them anyway.

We go home and it's as if we were returning from war, but from a war that isn't over. I think, We've become deserters. I think, We've become war correspondents, tourists. That's what we are, I think: tourists who arrive with their backpacks, their cameras, and their notebooks, prepared to spend a long time wearing out their eyes, but who suddenly decide to go home, and as they do they breathe a long sigh of relief.

A long relief, but a temporary one. Because in that feeling there is innocence and there is guilt, and although we can't and don't know how to talk about innocence or guilt, we spend our days going over a long list of things that back then, when we were children, we didn't know. It's as if we had witnessed a crime. We didn't commit it, we were only passing through the place, but we ran away because we knew that if they found us there we'd be blamed. We believe we are innocent, we believe we are guilty: we don't know.

Back home again Claudia looks at the shirts my father gave me. "I didn't have my own clothes for many years," she says suddenly. "First I used Ximena's castoffs, and then my mother's dresses. When she died we fought over everything, down to the last rag she left, and now I think maybe it was then that our relationship broke down for good. My father's suits, on the other hand, are still untouched in the closet in his room," she says.

I KEPT MY FATHER'S SHIRTS IN A DRAWER FOR months. In the meantime, many things have happened. In the meantime Claudia left and I started to write this book.

Now I look at those shirts, I spread them out on the bed. There is one I especially like, with an oil-blue color. I just tried it on, it's definitely too small. I look at myself in the mirror and I think how our parents' clothes should always be too big for us. But I also think I needed it; sometimes we need to wear our parents' clothes and look at ourselves for a long time in the mirror.

We never spoke honestly about that trip to Maipú. Many times I wanted to know what Claudia had felt, why she had wanted us to stay there, but every time I asked her, she answered me with excuses or stock phrases. Then came some long and silent days. Claudia seemed concentrated, busy and a little tense. I shouldn't have been surprised when she announced her decision. Supposedly I was expecting the end; supposedly there was no other ending possible.

"I've gone back to see Ximena," she said first, happily. She still hadn't agreed to sell the house, but they had renewed their relationship and that was much more important to Claudia than the inheritance. She told me they talked for hours, with no animosity of any kind. "Years ago, too many years ago now," she told me then, changing her tone in a way that seemed painful, "years ago I discovered I wanted a normal life. That I wanted, above all, to be calm. I already lived through emotions, all the emotions. I want a quiet, simple life. A life with walks in the park."

I thought about that half-casual, involuntary phrase: a life with walks in the park. I thought that my life was also, in a way, a life with walks in the park. But I understood what she meant. She was looking for a landscape of her own, a new park. A life where she was no longer anyone's daughter or sister. I insisted, I don't know why, I don't know for what. "You've reclaimed your past on this trip," I said.

"I don't know. But I've taken the opportunity to tell it to you. I took a trip back to my childhood that maybe I needed. But we shouldn't fool ourselves. Back then, when we were kids, you spied on my father because you wanted to be with me. It's the same thing now. You've listened to me just so you can see me. I know my story is important to you, but your own story is more important."

I thought that was hard, it was unfair. That she was saying unnecessary words. Suddenly I was furious, I even felt a hint of resentment. "You're very vain," I told her.

"Yes," she answered. "And so are you. You want me to back you up, to have the same opinions as you, like two teenagers who force coincidences in order to be together, and they narrow their view and lie."

I accepted the blow, maybe I deserved it. "I get it, you're leaving," I said. "Santiago is stronger than you. And Chile is a shitty country that's going to be run by a tycoon paying lip service to the bicentennial."

"I'm not leaving because of that," she said sharply.

"You're leaving because you're in love with someone else," I replied, as if it were a guessing game. I thought of her Argentine boyfriend and I also thought about Esteban, the blond boy who had been with her back then, in Maipú. I never asked if he was her boyfriend or not. I wanted to ask her now, too late, awkwardly, childishly. But before I could, she answered, emphatically: "I'm not in love with someone else." She took a long sip of coffee while she thought about what to say. "I'm not in love with anyone, really. If there's anything I'm sure of," she said, "it's that I'm not in love with anyone."

"But maybe it's better for you to think of it that way," she added later, in an indefinable tone. "It's easier to understand it that way. It's better for you to think that all this has been a love story."

WE'RE ALL RIGHT

THIS AFTERNOON EME FINALLY AGREED TO look at the manuscript. She didn't want me to read it out loud, the way I used to. She asked me to print the pages out and she covered herself with the sheet to read them in bed, but suddenly she changed her mind and started to get dressed. "I'd rather go home," she said. "I've been here a long time, I want to sleep in my own bed tonight."

I imagine her reading it now, in bed, in that house she has never invited me to visit. In that bed I don't know. My bed is hers as well, we picked it out together. And the sheets, the blankets, the comforter. I said as much to her before she left, but I wasn't expecting her answer: "For this to work," she said, "sometimes you have to pretend we've just met. That we've never shared anything before."

I was struck by the slightly forced restraint in her voice. She spoke to me the way one speaks to a man who complains unfairly in the supermarket line. "We're all in a hurry, sir. Be patient, wait your turn."

I'll wait for my turn, then. Sentimentally, respectfully.

»»»«««

At twenty years old, when I had just left home, I worked for a time counting cars. It was a simple and badly paid job, but in some ways I enjoyed sitting on my assigned corner and recording on the chart the number of cars, trucks, and buses that went by every hour. Most of all I liked the night shift, although sometimes I got sleepy and I'm sure I made an absurd picture: a young, distracted, haggard guy on a corner of Vicuña Mackenna, waiting for nothing, watching out of the corner of his eye as other young people returned home, boasting about their drunkenness.

It's night and I'm writing. That is my job now, or something like that. But as I write cars go by on Echeñique Avenue, and sometimes I get distracted and start counting them. In the past ten minutes fourteen cars have passed, three trucks, and one motorcycle. I can't tell if they turn at the next corner or if they keep going straight. In a vague, melancholy way I think I would like to know.

I think about the old Peugeot 404. My father used to spend weekends fixing it up, though it never actually broke down—he would say himself, with the particular love men have for cars, that it behaved well and had few problems. All the same, he spent his days tuning it up, changing its spark plugs, or reading until late from some chapter in *Apunto, the Automotive Encyclopedia*. I have never seen anyone as concentrated as my father was on those nights of reading.

I thought it was ridiculous for him to spend so much time on the car. Even worse, he made me help him—which consisted of waiting, with infinite patience, for him to finally say: "Pass me the crescent wrench." Then I had to wait for him to pass it back to me, and also listen to long explanations of mechanics that didn't interest me in the least. It was then I discovered there was a certain pleasure in the act of pretending to listen to my father or to other adults. In nodding my head and holding back the half smile of knowing I was thinking about something else.

The Peugeot's fate was a horrible one. An old truck going against traffic crashed into it, and my father almost died. I still remember when he showed me the mark the seat belt left on his chest. He was talking to me then about prudence, about the wisdom of rules. Suddenly he opened his shirt to show me the reddish mark that was drawn clearly on his dark chest. "If I hadn't put my seat belt on I'd be dead," he said.

The Peugeot was left in pieces and he had to sell it as scrap. I went with my father to the junkyard. Since then, every time I see a Peugeot 404 I remember that unsettling image. And also that mark, which I saw when we went to the pool or the beach. I didn't like to see my father in a bathing suit. I didn't like to see that mark cleaving his chest, that evidence, that horrible band that stayed on his body forever.

>>><<<

It's strange, it's silly to attempt a genuine story about something, about someone, about anyone, even oneself. But it's necessary as well.

It's four in the morning, I can't sleep. I get through the insomnia by counting cars and putting together new phrases on the refrigerator:

our perfect whisper
another white prostitute
understand strange picture
almost black mouth
how imagine howl
naked girl long rhythm

That last one is nice: naked girl long rhythm.

>>><<<

I arrived half an hour early, sat on the terrace, and ordered a glass of wine. I wanted to read while I waited for Eme, but some children were running dangerously around the tables, and it was hard to concentrate. They should be in school, I thought, but then I remembered it was Saturday.

I saw their mothers at the corner table, caught up in their trivial chatter.

She got there late. I noticed she seemed nervous, because she gave me a long explanation for the delay, as if she had never been late before. I thought she didn't want to talk about the novel, so I decided to ask her right away what she had thought of it. She searched a long time for the right tone. She stuttered. She tried to make a joke I didn't understand. "The novel is good," she said, finally. "It's a novel."

"What?"

"I said, it's a novel. I like it."

"But it isn't finished."

"But you will finish it and it'll be good."

I wanted to ask for more details, about some passages in particular, about certain characters, but it wasn't possible because one of the women from the corner table came over and greeted Eme effusively. "I'm Pepi," she said, and they hugged. I don't know if she said Pepi or Pepa or Pupo or Papo, but it was some nickname like that. She introduced us to her children, who were the loudest of the group. Eme could have cut the conversation off there, but she chose to keep on talking with her old classmate about what a huge coincidence it was to run into each other at that restaurant. It didn't seem like such a big coincidence to me. Pepi or Pupi or Papi lives in La Reina just like Eme. The strange thing is that they hadn't run into each other sooner.

I felt bad. I thought Eme was drawing out the con-

versation on purpose. That she was grateful for that en-
counter because it let her put off the moment when she
would have to give me a real opinion about the manuscript.
Then she said she was sorry and she had to go. I went home
frustrated, angry. I tried to go on writing, but I couldn't.

>>»«<<

When I was a child I liked the word *blackout*. My mother
would come get us and bring us into the living room. "In
the past, people didn't have electricity," she would say as
she lit the candles. It was hard for me to imagine a world
without lamps, without outlets in the walls.

Those nights, they let us stay up talking for a while and
my mother used to tell the joke about the candle that
couldn't be extinguished. It was long and boring, but we
liked it a lot: the family tried to put out a candle so they
could go to bed but they all had crooked mouths. Finally
the grandmother, who also had a crooked mouth, put out
the candle by wetting her fingers with saliva.

My father laughed at the joke, too. They were there so
we wouldn't feel afraid. But we weren't afraid. They were
the ones who were afraid.

That's what I want to talk about. *Those kinds of
memories.*

>>»«<<

Today my friend Pablo called me so he could read me this
phrase he found in a book by Tim O'Brien: "What sticks

to memory, often, are those odd little fragments that have no beginning and no end." I kept thinking about that and stayed awake all night. It's true. We remember the sounds of the images. And sometimes, when we write, we wash everything clean, as if by doing so we could advance toward something. We ought to simply describe those sounds, those stains on memory. That arbitrary selection, nothing more. That's why we lie so much, in the end. That's why a book is always the opposite of another immense and strange book. An illegible and genuine book that we translate treacherously, that we betray with our habit of passable prose.

I think about the beautiful beginning of *Family Sayings*, Natalia Ginzburg's novel: "The places, events, and people in this book are all real. I have invented nothing. Every time that I have found myself inventing something in accordance with my old habits as a novelist, I have felt impelled at once to destroy everything thus invented."

»»»«««

I'm in Las Cruces, enjoying the empty beach, with Eme.

In the morning, stretched out in the sand, I read *Promise at Dawn*, the book by Romain Gary where this precise, opportune paragraph appears: "I don't know how to speak of the sea. I only know that it frees me for the moment from all my burdens. Every time I look at it I become a happy drowned man."

I don't know how to speak of the sea either, although it was presumably the first landscape I saw. When I was barely two months old my father took a job in Valparaíso and we went to live on Cerro Alegre for three years. But my first memory of the sea is much later, at perhaps six years old, when we were already living in Maipú. I remember thinking, awestruck and happy, that it was a limitless space, that the sea was a place that continued, that kept on going.

I've just tried to write a poem called "The Happy Drowned." It didn't work out.

>>><<<

We returned in a car Eme borrowed. I drove so carefully that I think she started to get desperate. Then I went with her, for the first time, to her house. I was struck by seeing her things dispersed in new ways. Recognizable. I don't know if I liked sleeping there with her. I spent the whole time overwhelmed by the need to take in every detail.

In the morning we had tea with her friends. It was just as Eme had described it to me. The house is really an immense workshop. While Eme draws, her housemates— she has used their names many times but I can never remember them—make clothes and handicrafts.

When I was about to leave Eme asked me if I was writing. I didn't know how to answer.

In any case, last night I wrote these lines:

It's better not to be in any book
for the words not to try to protect us
A life with no music and no lyrics
and a sky without the clouds you see there now

>>»«««

My prose turns out odd. I can't find the humor, the frame of mind. But I come up with some iambic lines and suddenly I let that rhythm take over. I move the lines, reinforce and break the cadence. I spend hours working on the poem. I read, out loud:

It's better not to be in any book
for the words not to try to protect us
A life with no music and no lyrics
and a sky without the clouds you see there now
The clouds—you hardly know if they are coming
closer or retreating when they alter
their shapes so often and you'd hardly know
we weren't still living in the place we left behind
before we understood even the names
of the trees
before we understood even the names
of the birds
When fear was only fear and there was no
love of fear
or fear of fear
and pain was an interminable book

that we once looked through quickly just in case
our names might be there in it at the end

>>>««

I dreamed that I was drunk and I was dancing to a song by Los Ángeles Negros, "The Train to Forgetting." Suddenly Alejandra Costamagna appeared. "You're really wasted," she was saying, "I'd better take you home, give me your address." But I had forgotten my address and I kept dancing while I tried to remember it. In the dream I was drinking pisco and Coke; in the dream I liked pisco and Coke.

Alejandra was dancing with me but it was more like her way of helping me. I stumbled around outrageously, I almost fell down in the middle of the dance floor. But it wasn't the dance floor of a club; it was someone's living room.

"We aren't friends," I said to Alejandra in the dream. "Why are you helping me if we aren't friends?"

"Because we *are* friends," she answered. "You're dreaming and in the dream you think we aren't friends. But we *are* friends. Try to wake up," she said. I tried, but I stayed in the dream and I started to get anxious.

Finally I woke up. Eme was sleeping next to me. I called Alejandra, told her about the dream. She laughed. "I like that song," she said.

She asked how things were going with Eme. "I don't know," I answered instinctively. And it's true, I think now: I don't know.

>>»«««

There is pain but also happiness when you give up on a book. It's felt that way to me, at least: first there's the melodrama of having wasted so many nights on a useless passion. But then, as the days pass, a slight, favorable wind prevails. We start to feel comfortable again in that room where we write without any greater purpose, with no precise goal.

We give up on a book when we realize that it wasn't for us. From wanting to read it so badly we believed it was up to us to write it. We were tired of waiting for someone to write the book that we wanted to read.

I don't plan to give up on my novel, though. Eme's silence wounds me and I understand why. I made her read the manuscript, and now I want to make her accept it. And the weight of her possible disapproval makes me wish I hadn't written it, or to give up on it. But no. I'm not going to give up on it.

>>»«««

I had planned to have lunch with my parents, but the prospect of watching them celebrate Piñera's victory discourages me. I call them and tell them I won't be coming out to vote. On the bus I listen to very good songs, but suddenly music, any music, becomes unbearable. I put my headphones away and I start reading *Promise at Dawn*. I'm transfixed by this line: "Instead of howling, I write books."

I vote with a sense of sorrow, with very little faith. I know that Sebastián Piñera will win the first round and I'm sure he will also win the second. It seems horrible. It's obvious we've lost our memories. We will calmly, candidly, hand the country over to Piñera and to Opus Dei and the Legionaries of Christ.

After voting I call my friend Diego. I wait for him a long time, sitting on the grass in the plaza, close to the pool. We take the long walk to the Maipú Temple, and we pass by the place where the Toqui supermarket used to be. Diego is from Iquique but he's lived in Maipú for ten years. "The deli and the bakery were good," I tell him, and I describe the supermarket in detail. He listens respectfully, but it's possible he thinks my interest is ridiculous, since supermarkets are all the same.

"I've never been to the temple before," says Diego. We go inside in the middle of one of the many Sunday masses. There aren't many people. We sit near the altar. I look at the little flags, I count them. Afterward we sit on the stairs of the entrance and we can hear the mass over the loudspeaker. We talk while some kids play soccer, and every once in a while they kick the ball close to us. I hurry to kick it back, but suddenly one of them kicks the ball hard and it hits Diego in the face. We expect them to apologize or at least to smile apologetically. They don't. I sit there holding the ball, the kids come over, they take it from my hands. I'm furious. I want to scold them. To raise them right.

We talk about Maipú, about the Chilean idea of a villa, so different from the Argentine or Spanish one. The dream of the middle class, but a middle class without rituals, without roots. I ask him if he remembers a soap opera on Channel 13 called *Villa Nápoli*. Diego doesn't remember. Sometimes I forget that he is much younger than me.

We talk about my novel, but also about the novel Diego published recently and that I read a few weeks before. I tell him I liked it; I try to explain why I liked it. I think of one scene in particular. The protagonist travels to Buenos Aires with his father and asks him for a book. The father buys it for him and, to show his approval, he opens it and says, "It's sturdy."

"You didn't make that up," I say to him. "That's the kind of thing you don't make up." Diego laughs, shaking his head as if he were dancing to heavy metal. "No, I didn't make it up," he says.

Then we go to the apartment where Diego lives with his mother, in Avenida Sur. His mother's name is Cinthya. We talk about the results, which by that hour of the afternoon are already clear. Second round, with a huge advantage for Piñera.

Diego prepares the avocado and adds oil. I tell him avocado doesn't need oil. "My dad always gets on me for that too," he says, and laughs.

"At least your dad has *that* right," I answer, and I laugh, too.

>>»>«««

"I thought you were joking when you said you were writing about me," Eme told me in the restaurant. She looked at me as if searching for my face. I felt that she was choosing her words carefully. That she was getting ready to talk. But she stopped at a smile.

We went to eat sushi at the same place as always. Our order took longer than it should have and I remembered the lunch scene when I was a child—the anguish of leaving with the food on the table. "It's like in the novel," I was going to say to her, but she was looking at me with extinguished curiosity. Now I think she was looking at me with compassion. I thought we were approaching that period of the wait when the only possible topic of conversation is the wait. But she began another conversation, with a tone that she seemed to have thought about, that she surely had been practicing at length for days.

"I haven't changed that much," she said. "And neither have you. Some weeks ago I told you we should pretend we have just met. I don't understand very well what I wanted to say to you. I think that during these months we've been laughing at what we used to be. But it's false. We're still what we used to be. Now we understand everything. But we know very little. We know less than before . . ."

"But that's a good thing," I said fearfully. "It's good not to know, not to expect more."

"No. It isn't good. It would be good if it were real. We want to be together and so we're prepared even to pretend. We haven't changed so much that we can be together again. And I wonder if we're going to change."

I understood what was coming and I readied myself. In arguments I tended to take refuge in a certain optimism, but she would close her face and then even her body to keep me out. I'll always remember the pain, one night, years ago: in the middle of an argument we started caressing each other and she got on top of me, but in the middle of penetration she couldn't control her rage and she shut her vagina completely.

Suddenly, unexpectedly, Eme started talking about the novel. She had liked it, but throughout her reading she couldn't avoid an ambiguous feeling, a hesitation. "You told my story," she said, "and I ought to thank you, but no, I think I'd prefer it if no one told that story." I explained that it wasn't exactly her life, and that I had only taken some images, some memories we had shared. "Don't make excuses," she said. "You left some cash in the safe but you still robbed the bank." It struck me as a silly, vulgar metaphor.

The sushi arrived, finally. I focused on the salmon sashimi—I ate voraciously, putting too much soy sauce on each piece and letting the ginger and wasabi burn my mouth. It was as if I wanted to punish myself absurdly while thinking how I loved this woman, how it was a complete love and not a worn-out way of loving. How she wasn't a habit for me, not a vice that was hard to give up. And nevertheless, at that point I wasn't, I'm not, willing to fight anymore.

I ate the sushi, my pieces and hers as well, and when the tray was empty Eme said to me dryly, "Let's call this off now." Just then the manager arrived and began a lengthy apology that neither of us wanted to listen to. He offered us free coffee and dessert on the house to make up for the wait. We listened to him absently. We answered mechanically that it didn't matter, he shouldn't worry. And we left, each going our separate way.

When I got home I thought about Eme's words. I thought she was right. That we know very little. That we used to know more, because we were full of conviction, dogma, rules. That we loved those rules. That the only thing we had really loved was that absurd handful of rules. And now we understand everything. We understand, especially, failure.

Alone again (naturally). What hurts the most is that *naturally*. Let us go, then, you and I, each our separate way.

>>»«<<

A few days ago Eme left a box for me with the neighbors. Only today did I dare open it. There were two shirts, a scarf, my Kaurismäki and Wes Anderson movies, my Tom Waits and Wu-Tang Clan CDs, as well as some books I lent her these past months. Among them there was also the copy of *In Praise of Shadows*, the essay by Tanizaki, that I gave her years ago. I don't know if it was out of cruelty or carelessness that she put it in the box.

She never told me she had read it, so I was surprised to recognize in the book, just now, the marks she made with a thick yellow highlighter. I used to berate her for that: her books looked awful after the battle that was her reading. One would think she read with the anxiety of a student memorizing dates for a test, but no, she was just in the habit of marking the phrases that she liked that way.

I speak in the past tense of Eme. It's sad and easy: she isn't here anymore. But I should also learn to speak in the past tense about myself.

»»»«««

I've gone back to the novel. I try out changes. From first to third person, from third to first, even to second.

I move toward and away from the narrator. And I don't get anywhere. I'm not going to get anywhere. I change scenes. I delete. I delete a lot. Twenty, thirty pages. I forget about this book. I get drunk little by little, I fall asleep.

And then when I wake up I write verses, and I realize that was everything: to remember the images fully, no compositions of place, no unnecessary scenes. To find a genuine music. No more novels, no more excuses.

I experiment with erasing everything to allow that rhythm, those words, to prevail:

The table swallowed up in tongues of fire
The scars that showed on my father's body
The quick confidence amid the rubble
The phrases written on the childhood wall
The sound of my restless drumming fingers
Your clothes in some other house's drawers
The never-ending sound of passing cars
The warm, steady hope of a return
Without steps or paths of memory
The firm conviction that what we hope for
Is that no one will see in our faces
The faces we relinquished long ago

≫≫≫≪≪≪

Weeks without writing in this diary. The whole summer, almost.

I was awake, unable to sleep, listening to the Magnetic Fields, when the earthquake began. I sat in a doorway and I thought, calmly and with a strange serenity, that it was the end of the world. It's long, I also thought. I managed to think that many times: it was long.

When it finally ended I went over to check on the neighbors, a married couple and their little girl, who all still had their arms around one another, trembling. "Is everyone okay?"

"We're fine," answered the neighbor. "Just a little scared. And how are you two?" he asked.

I answered him, surprised: "We're fine."

I've lived alone for two years and my neighbor doesn't know, I thought. I also thought that now *I* was the single neighbor, now *I* was Raúl, *I* was Roberto. Then I remembered the novel. Alarmed, I believed the story would end like that: with the house in Maipú, my childhood home, destroyed. What had made me write about the earthquake of 1985? I didn't know, I don't know. I do know, though, that on that long-ago night I thought about death for the first time.

Back then death was invisible for children like me, who went outside, running fearlessly along those fantastical streets, safe from history. The night of the earthquake was the first time I realized that everything could come tumbling down. Now I think it's a good thing to know. It's necessary to remember it every second.

Past five in the morning I went out to look around the neighborhood. I walked slowly, waiting for the help lent by flashlight beams bouncing confusedly from the ground up to the treetops, and by headlights that would suddenly fill the night. Children slept or were trying to sleep stretched out on the sidewalk. A masculine voice reassured, from one corner to the next, like a mantra: We're all right, we're all right.

I turned on my phone radio. Information was still scarce. The inventory of deaths was slowly beginning. The announcers were faltering, and one even uttered a sentence that, under the circumstances, was comical: "This has definitely been an earthquake."

Finally, I ended up near Eme's house, and I stayed on the sidewalk, waiting for some sign. Suddenly I heard her voice. She was talking to her friends; they must have been smoking in the front yard. I was going to go over to them, but then I thought that it was enough for me to know she was safe. I felt her close by, a few steps away, but I decided to leave immediately. We're all right, I thought, with a strange flicker of happiness.

I returned home at dawn. I was struck by the scene when I went inside. Some days earlier I had organized my books. Now they were a generous ruin on the floor. Same for the plates and two windows. The house had survived, though.

I thought about going immediately to Maipú, but just before nine in the morning I managed to reach my mother.

"We're all right," she said, and she asked me not to come see them, saying the trip out there was very dangerous. "Stay home and organize your books," she said. "Don't worry about us."

But I'm going to go. Early tomorrow I'm going to see them, I'm going to be with them.

It's late. I'm writing. The city is convalescing, but little by little the sounds of any other end-of-summer night are resuming. I think naively, intensely, about suffering. About the people who died today, in the south. About yesterday's dead, and tomorrow's. And about this profession, this strange, humble and arrogant, necessary and insufficient trade: to spend life watching, writing.

After the Peugeot 404 my father had a light blue 504 and then a silver 505. None of those models are out on the avenue tonight.

I watch the cars, I count the cars. It's overwhelming to think that in the backseats children are sleeping, and that every one of those children will remember, someday, the old car they rode in years before, with their parents.